Random Letters

& other short stories.

Lois Francis

Random Letters & other short stories

First published in 2024 by
Lois Francis

ISBN: 9798342449861

This is a complementary book provided for guests of Galtres Retreat Lodges.
www.galtresretreatlodges.co.uk

Guests may purchase a personal copy from Amazon.co.uk

Introduction

First of all, thank you for picking up this copy of Random Letters and Other Short Stories.

In a previous existence I was a therapist and lecturer and I wrote a number of books, teaching materials, text books and self-help books, inspired by my work with my patients.

On retirement I decided that I would turn my hand to writing short stories and even published another self-help book, heavily disguised as a novel!

I decided it was high time I shared my short story writing with a wider audience and so this book came into being. It's a random collection of stories, with no particular theme, so you might find one that you enjoy within it's pages. Some of the stories have a basis in actual events in the lives of family members or myself. Others – well they're complete figments of my imagination. I'll leave you to decide which is which, but there are no prizes for accurate guessing!

Enjoy!

Best wishes

Lois Francis.

P.S. If you'd like to have your own copy of this book at home, please order it from Amazon.co.uk.

Contents

Random Letters

I bet you've seen it yourself if you've been on Facebook "it deson't mttaer in waht oredr the ltteers in a wrod aepapr, the olny iprmoatnt tihng is taht the frist and lsat ltteer are in the rghit pcale. The rset can be a toatl mses and you can sitll raed it wouthit pobelrm."

I patted myself on the back when I read it, thinking I must be so clever to be able to translate this to "it doesn't matter in what order the letters in a word appear, the only important thing is that the first and last letter are in the right place." But no, it seems that everyone's brain is a virtual code cracking machine.

But I digress, I guess you're wondering where I'm going with this. It all started when Pete went to work in Dubai. I could have gone with him and taken our 10 year old son, Alex, but we agreed that it wasn't the kind of environment we wanted our child to be in. So, Pete goes off for 3 months at a time and I stay home to look after Alex.

My day is now divided into distinct chunks. Get up, shower and dress. Get Alex's breakfast ready whilst he decides whether or not he's going to grace the world with his presence. The smell of bacon or toast wafting up the stairs usually cracks his determination to stay in bed as long as possible. Heaven knows what he's going to be like when he's a teenager. I did read that one head teacher, recognising that teenager's body clocks work differently to normal adults, pushed back the school starting time by an hour to give the poor little loves time to become functioning humans.

But I digress, something I've honed to a fine art lately. After breakfast I walk with Alex to school. Kissing him at the school gates in now strictly forbidden. I have to stop a minimum of 6 metres away from him the moment he sees one of his pals and give him an off-hand wave, which I've now perfected. Blowing kisses is also strictly forbidden as is telling him "have a nice day, darling."

I'm now free to get on with the next chunk of my day, which may be go to the local Costa with a couple of friends or go to the yoga/pilates (annoyingly referred to as Yogalates) class in the church hall next to the school. On the days that Yogalates is not on and I don't go to Costa, I trudge home to set about cleaning the house and thinking about what culinary delight I can tempt Alex with that night. Thankfully, he's not a picky eater and enjoys his food. We've got into the habit of cooking and eating together before he does his homework.

No Yogalates or Costa also means that when I'm done with cleaning I can practise some yoga at home. This is the next chunk and my favourite hour of the day. I roll out my mat, pull on my yoga gear and put a relaxing "new age" CD on to play. I love the stretching, the rhythmic movements of Sun Salutations, upward dog, downward dog, trikonarsana, parvotonasana... I'd love to be able to reel off more of the Ashtanga Yoga series names, but I can only remember a few and that most of them begin with P. Ah well, thankfully I have a poster on the wall to help me remember the sequence and I finish with a few minutes of quiet meditation. That's when I'm not wondering how Pete is doing in Dubai, if Alex is okay at school and what on earth am I going to do to fill the rest of the day and the long evening ahead.

Next chunk, brain training. There's a website with lots of different games designed to stretch the brain. I like the word games best, mainly because I don't get on with Sudoku.

I look at Samurai Sudoku and hastily click away to Word Zap. Immediately I see "What are you?"

What??? I click on a new game and see "doing whit your plan?"

What plan? This is just a coincidence of random letters appearing in the game. Isn't it?

Time runs out on the game, so I start a new one. And what do I see? "Learn, teach, yoga."

WHAT???

I'm a bit freaked out by now. Yes, before I had Alex I wanted to train as a yoga teacher, but I can think of a 1001 reasons why it's too late. I'm responsible for running our home, keeping everything ticking over till Pete gets back from Dubai. Looking after Alex…….

I shake my head and click on a different game Word Ruffle. You have to try and make as many 3, 4, 5 and 6 letter words as you can out of the letters. I click on a new game. There in front of me are 6 random letters – and the 6 letter word is COWARD.

Right, I've had enough of this. Time for the next chunk of the day.

I phone my Mum. "What's up love? You sound a bit rattled? Are you okay?"

"Yes, yes," I respond "just missing Pete".

"Hmmm, I think your problem is that you've put your life on hold for Pete and Alex. I remember a time when you had lots of ideas, plans……"

I could tell I was in for a long lecture, so I hastily made up an excuse and grabbing my coat, I rushed out the door to school. Of course, I was far too early. The teachers didn't get to return our little darlings for a least another hour. Costa called me.

I sat deep in thought, reflecting on the word zap game, was I really a coward? Had I put my life on hold? I was only brought back to reality by my friend joining me for as she put it "a last few minutes of sanity before we collect the monsters." I told her about my weird experience that afternoon and she surprised me by saying she thought I'd be a good yoga teacher.

After dinner that evening Alex and I sat together to play Bananagrams. You're supposed to play opposite each other, but I want to encourage his wordsmith skills, so we play as a team.

Perhaps you know the game? You start with 21 random letters and you have to turn them into a crossword grid. As you pick more letters you can re-arrange the ones you have till you've used up all the letters.

Alex spilled the first 21 letter tiles onto the table. And perfectly arranged in front of me was

"taech, yog, trian, laern, now" which, of course, you know reads "teach yoga train learn now"

Well, what could I do? I was clearly being pushed to do something that's been on my mind for years. And so, here I am, leading my own yoga classes. My time isn't broken down into chunks any more just to get me through the day. I have a life outside of my relationships and purpose.

Mind   you,   I've   stopped   playing   word   zap.

A Random Act of Kindness

It was Remembrance Day, 11th November. Lorna was wearing her poppy with pride in honour of the men and women who had fought for the freedom she enjoyed. It had seemed a strange date for a concert when she'd booked the tickets months before, but she'd shrugged her shoulders and bought them anyway. The group they were going to see had been off the radar for 20 or more years, yet their music had been a huge source of comfort and inspiration to Lorna when she had been going through a difficult time in her life.

Determined not to dwell on the past, Lorna and her husband drove into Birmingham City late in the afternoon so that they could enjoy a meal by the canal side near Symphony Hall. She was still using a stick, having only had hip replacement surgery a few weeks previously. They strolled from the car park to one of their favourite restaurants and asked the maître D to give them comfortable seats in the warm. They were ushered to a long red leather banquette and a table for 4 where she was able to shrug off her winter coat, scarf and gloves and rest her stick at her side.

They chatted a while, pleased to be out of the house and enjoying the warm, convivial atmosphere of the restaurant. They had given themselves plenty of time before the concert, so decided to order drinks and some olives before ordering a starter. They were nibbling some olives when a waiter ushered an elderly gentleman to the table for two which was next to them. "I'm sorry we don't have your usual table. Will this table be alright for you tonight?" the waiter asked. "Yes,

yes it's fine thank you" the old man replied as he took off his winter coat and hung it on the back of a chair before settling himself on the banquette just a little way from Lorna.

Her husband was checking his phone for the latest news headlines, so Lorna indulged herself in some people watching. She noticed how the old man had hung his coat very carefully on the back of the chair so that the hem didn't trail on the floor. He was wearing beige trousers, a cream shirt and beige checked jacket with a checked tie. His shoes were caramel coloured and even his socks were cream, co-ordinating with his outfit. Lorna looked up into bright blue eyes and silver hair which was neatly brushed back. She couldn't help but notice how thin the old man was. He didn't seem to have a scrap of spare flesh on him, yet he didn't seem frail at all. On the contrary, his eyes showed an alert intelligence, his movements precise and measured.

Lorna was fascinated. Who was he? Someone's husband, father, grandfather? Perhaps he was meeting someone for dinner? The waiter returned and the old man ordered a glass of merlot and "just a starter today, I'll have the pate." He looked vaguely familiar, but she couldn't place where she might have seen him before.

She returned to their conversation, her husband sharing with her the latest political news about the forthcoming election. They chatted idly about the concert and what the Lighthouse Family had been doing in their 20 year absence, for this was the group they were going to see. The starters arrived and for a while Lorna was absorbed in enjoying her food. When the waiter cleared the plates they told him they would order a main course shortly.

No longer distracted by eating, Lorna saw that the old man's pate and wine had been brought to him. How delicately he sipped his wine before starting to eat the pate. A tiny amount of butter was spread on the toasted bread and an equally small amount of pate. Then a tiny bite of the toast, before it was returned to the plate and the old man opened his newspaper, spreading it out across his table before he began to read.

The main course was ordered and was served in almost record time. Beef Bourguignon for her husband and Poulet Breton for Lorna. She began to eat and out of the corner of her eye saw the old man repeat his actions of earlier. A tiny amount of butter on the toasted bread, a tiny amount of pate and tiny bites. She began to feel rather greedy as she hungrily ate her meal. "No wonder he's so thin" she thought "if he can make a meal of a starter." And yet she began to feel sorry for him, perhaps he couldn't afford more than a starter, perhaps he had a medical condition where he could only eat small meals, but he didn't look ill, far from it.

The old man seemed oblivious to her interest, turning the pages of his paper, quietly reading. It was only when she returned her own reading glasses to her bag after studying the dessert menu that she realized he wasn't wearing glasses although he seemed to be reading the paper with ease.

Lorna's interest in him was piqued. The waiters left him alone although they clearly knew him. Was he a military veteran? Was he alone in life with no family to care about him? His dress and demeanor were of a bygone age. He looked up and caught her eye, they exchanged smiles and he returned to his newspaper.

Here was a man who, although sitting in this restaurant and eating on his own maintained standards. Again, she noticed how thin he was, by comparison she felt huge, though most would say she was slim. She felt an urge to do something for him, his military bearing reminded her of all those who had lost their lives fighting for their country, including her own son. Determined not to spoil the evening, she turned back to her husband and smiled, a shadow of sadness on her face.

When it came time to pay their bill the old man was still slowly nibbling his toast and pate, sipping his wine. The manager brought the bill and Lorna remembered that she had a voucher to redeem. It was on her phone, so she handed it over to the manager who took it with him to the cash desk.

Seeing her opportunity Lorna quickly followed, ostensibly to retrieve her phone and asked the manager "The old man at the table next to us. Does he come here often, you seem to know him?" "Oh yes" replied the manager "he comes quite often, he likes to have a glass of wine and relax while he reads the paper. Why? Is there a problem?" he asked with a concerned expression on his face. "No, not at all, I'd like to pay his bill. Please don't tell him it was me, just say it's an early Christmas present. Don't tell him until we have left. I'll pay my bill while I'm here."

And so it was done, she'd felt teary eyed when she said she wanted to pay his bill but then there was a warm glow inside.

Lorna went to the toilet and returned to her table, sliding alongside the old man as she returned to her seat. She couldn't help but notice that he'd removed his shoes and his stockinged feet were resting on them. Her husband got up to use the toilet before they left and she turned to the old man. "It's so nice to find somewhere where you can sit and relax for a while isn't it?"

"Oh yes" he replied "I like it here. It's warm and there's a good light to read my paper by. Do you come here often yourself?"

"We do when we're in Birmingham, we've driven over from Coventry to see a concert at Symphony Hall."

"That's nice, it'll be good when the trams are running in a couple of months, it will make it much easier to get here from the station."

They chatted for a minute or two more and she began to pull her scarf and coat on ready to leave. He helped her with her coat and as she left she turned and said "enjoy the rest of your evening."

As they were walking out of the restaurant the manager gave her a beaming smile "you've made my day, that was really sweet of you." Her husband asked what she had done and she told him. "That was nice, he can come again and have a glass of wine and a starter another day."

Lorna lay in bed later that night and thought about the old man. Had he been pleased that his bill had been paid? She would never know and somehow it didn't matter.

The Major

David looked in the mirror in the hall, before reaching for his keys and his coat. He pulled his shoulders back and stood straight as he checked that his tie had been knotted correctly and his hair was combed. He wasn't a vain man, even though at 80 he could still be considered good looking with his bright blue eyes and silver hair. Standards had to be maintained.

He smiled as he remembered how Alice used to tease him. "You're not in the army now you know, I won't walk 10 paces behind you if you're not wearing a tie." But no, standards had to be maintained. It was a hard habit to break, even if he'd wanted to. He certainly wasn't going to dress like the youth of today with their baggy, ripped jeans and hoodies. He sighed as he remembered the rigours of army life, the uniform inspections and the drill sergeant shouting his orders on the parade ground. "A couple of years in the army would sort some of these youths out, pity they scrapped National Service" he thought as he carefully locked the door behind him and left the house.

It was Remembrance Day and as David walked into town many people were wearing poppies. In New Street station there was an Armed Forces band and singers and he stopped and listened to them for a while. His gaze wandered around the faces of the servicemen and women, seeing how young they were and he was reminded of his former comrades.

He'd been a major when the Falklands war had started. It had been a brief but bloody conflict and he'd lost many men. He could remember their faces still and sometimes in the dead of night he would think about them. He especially remembered one young man's heroism, it seemed so pointless now, what difference had his death made? All those people wearing poppies, it was easy for them to remember one day a year, for him it was every day. So many lives lost, families left without a husband, a father, a son. He knew he'd been lucky to make it home uninjured.

David shook his head and walked briskly on. "No good brooding about the past, can't bring them back" he told himself, though how he wished he could bring Alice back. Even after 5 years he could see her face clearly and sometimes he caught sight of someone in the crowds who looked just like her. They say that time is a great healer, but for David the pain was as acute as the day Alice had died in his arms. They hadn't been lucky enough to have children, it had just been him and Alice. It hadn't mattered whilst she was alive, but now, he was so lonely.

There were neighbours who kept an eye out for him but there was no-one who genuinely cared about him. No-one who would miss him when he was dead. What was he waiting for when he could be re-united with Alice? Funnily enough the staff at the restaurant were almost like friends. They always greeted him warmly when he went in and sat him at his favourite table, it was the one that he and Alice always shared.

It was almost a ritual now, going to the restaurant reminded him of Alice and in a strange way it felt as though she were near. He bought a copy of the evening newspaper and walked briskly through the streets of Birmingham toward the restaurant. David was dismayed to see a couple sitting at "his" table. "We're sorry sir, will this table be alright tonight?" asked the waiter as he led him to the next table along the banquette. "Yes, yes, it's fine" he said as he shrugged off his coat. He carefully hung the coat on the back of the chair facing him and sat down. Glancing sideways he could see a woman in her sixties, a walking stick rested at her side. Hmm, he supposed he could let her have his table for tonight.

David settled back and perused the menu. He took his time studying it though he knew exactly what he would have, he was a creature of habit. "A glass of Merlot and just a starter today please, I'll have the pate" he said when the waiter came back to take his order. He opened his newspaper and began to read, pleased that there was enough light to read by. He was quietly pleased that even at 80 he didn't need to wear reading glasses, though he noticed the woman next to him had to use them to read her menu. He couldn't help overhearing snatches of the couple's conversation. They were discussing the forthcoming election and the concert they were going to.

David's mind drifted back to the many concerts he'd been to with Alice. They favoured classical music and had seen many great concerts in their day. He chuckled to himself as he remembered one time when they'd been to the Royal Albert Hall for a classic spectacular which ended with the 1812 overture. They'd had seats in one of the top tiers and Alice hadn't noticed the big cannon on the very top level. She'd almost fallen over the balcony she'd jumped so much when the cannon had fired. But then she'd been like an excited child, loving the muskets, cannons and fireworks. It had been worth the trip to London for that concert just to see her pleasure. There wouldn't be any more concerts for him now, it wasn't the same to go on your own. He idly wondered who the Lighthouse Family were, "strange name for a group" he thought, "mind the Beatles was a strange name too."

When his pate arrived he spread a little of the toast with butter and pate. He'd learned over the past few years that small bites, chewed thoroughly made it last longer. That meant longer to sit in the warmth of the restaurant, reading his paper. He kicked off his shoes and settled his stockinged feet on top of them, wiggling his toes. It was colder out than he'd anticipated and it was nice to sit back and relax and let his feet warm up.

The couple next to him had already eaten a starter and were enjoying a main course. David resolutely ate tiny morsels of his toast and pate. He'd perfected the art of chewing very slowly and letting his taste buds enjoy every last bit of his food. There wouldn't be a main course for him, or a dessert, the budget would only allow for a glass of wine and a starter, but just for once, a Poulet Breton would be nice.

David looked up from time to time and exchanged a brief smile with the woman seated next to him. He noticed a sadness in her smile and her eyes. She reminded him of the woman he'd been to see some 20 years previously. Her son had died saving his comrade but he knew it was of no consolation to her, it would never bring back her beloved son. He guessed she would be about the same age as the woman sitting next to him now.

He was engrossed in his newspaper when he noticed the woman follow the waiter to the cash desk. The waiter had her mobile phone and she followed him to retrieve it. There was some discussion at the cash desk between the woman and the head waiter, who looked across at him before speaking to the woman again. David shrugged his shoulders, it was nothing to do with him.

The woman spent a couple of minutes paying her bill and disappeared in the direction of the toilets. When she came back to the table she told the man with her that she had paid the bill. "Oh, okay, I'll just go to the toilet before we leave." The woman turned toward David, fussing with her scarf. "It's so nice to find somewhere where you can sit and relax for a while isn't it?" she said to David as he looked up at her. "Oh yes" he replied "I like it here. It's warm and there's a good light to read my paper by. Do you come here often yourself?"

"We do when we're in Birmingham, we've driven over from Coventry to see a concert at Symphony Hall" she replied as she began to pull on her coat. David reached across and helped her with the coat, handing the walking stick to her as she stood up to leave. "Enjoy the rest of your evening" she said giving him a warm smile as she walked over to her husband.

David noticed the restaurant manager beaming at her and patting her arm as she joined her husband. "What was that all about?" he wondered idly and then turned back to his newspaper.

David thought about the woman for a moment and wondered why she'd seemed so familiar. She'd had a lovely smile and reminded him of Alice. Alice who had loved him and cared about him every day through their married life. He quickly brushed away a tear, "you can stop that David, no feeling sorry for yourself just because you think no-one cares about you anymore." He picked up his wineglass and finished the last few drops of wine. "Cheers, here's to you my love, I miss you so much, but hopefully I'll be seeing you again soon."

A few minutes later the head waiter came over. He had a beaming smile on his face, "your bill tonight sir, it's been paid. An early Christmas present the lady said." David was taken by surprise "what do you mean, it's been paid?" "Just that sir, it's a gift from another customer, your bill is paid. Can I get you anything else?"

David sat back, he didn't know what to say. Who had paid his bill? Why? Who had cared enough about a lonely old man to pay for his meal? He blinked rapidly, no tears, that would never do. He realized he would never know who had paid the bill and that it didn't really matter. "I'll have another glass of wine and I think I'll have a main course tonight please" he said with smile.

April Fool

I woke early and could feel my heart racing. This was it, the day my carefully made plans were put into action. Trying to stay calm, I did a few sun salutations before heading to the bathroom for a shower. When I'd moved into the spare room months ago, Simon hadn't objected and we hadn't had sex in over a year. I guess he didn't need to have sex with me when he was shagging his mistress at every opportunity.

Crossing the landing, the sound of the shower in the en-suite told me that Simon was up and getting ready to leave.

"Breathe, take deep breaths and you'll get through the next few hours." I reassured myself.

When Simon emerged, freshly showered and dressed in one of his Saville Row suits I handed him a freshly brewed cup of coffee, cooled to the right temperature. Past mistakes had taught me not to hand him scalding hot coffee. He'd given up the toast and marmalade a while back "got to look after my heart" he'd said at the time, patting his developing paunch. More like his mistress had told him to lose weight, I'd thought.

"I've got your case packed as you asked. Your best suits, shirts and casual wear. I know you want to make a good impression with the guys in Singapore." My voice shook a little, praying he wouldn't find fault and lash out one last time before he left.

"Have a good trip, I hope your flight is on time. The car will be here in a minute to take you to the airport."

"Yes, yes, I'll see you when I get back." He no longer bothered with a perfunctory kiss on the cheek, for which small mercy I was grateful. I'd been madly in love with him at one time, but his selfishness, quick temper and refusal to start a family had killed it. The final death knell on our marriage had been when he'd left his phone unlocked and I saw the messages he'd been sending his mistress. "It won't be long now, I'll get it all sorted while we're in Singapore. She'll be glad to get the house and we'll be moving into our new home when we get back."

That had been a couple of months ago. For a clever man, he was surprising naïve about internet security. I'd had a feeling that he'd been smuggling, exactly what, I wasn't sure, but there on his computer in his browsing history was all the information I'd needed to bring him down.

He'd been totally dismissive when I'd started my web design company, even though I'd made a great job of building a website for his company.

Perhaps I'd known then that the end was in sight, as I'd reverted to using my maiden name. Portia Parkinson was a bit of a mouthful, so PP Web Design had seemed a good name. Our solicitor had recommended his bank where I set up an account for my business. I'd also created a PP Client Account for holding client's deposit money, which was going to be key to the success of my plans.

As soon as the limousine had disappeared I raced up the stairs to his office and fired up his computer. Hands shaking, I logged into his personal email account and checked for the hundredth time the emails from our solicitor, Peter Parker.

15th March.

"Thank you for the deposit money received today, I shall proceed with the purchase and aim for completion on 3rd April. I confirm that I have registered the title to your current property in your wife's name. I have the title deed from HMLR which I will send to her on 3rd April with your accompanying letter, as instructed."

Of course, I already knew that the house had been transferred to my name, £3 spent with HMLR had been a good investment.

Now all I had to do was wait for Peter Parker to request completion funds from Simon and then I could send my own email. It had been deliciously easy to register a web address PeterParkerSolicitors.co and create an email address almost exactly the same as his, Peter@PeterParker.co Simon would never notice that one tiny detail, the missing .uk.

An hour crawled by reviewing the correspondence between Simon and Peter Parker. They were so damned arrogant, convinced that I was the dumb little wife who played at making pretty websites.

After a couple of hours I was thirsty and desperate for a pee. A quick bathroom visit and armed with a coffee, I returned to the computer and checked incoming emails. Nothing yet.

19

Simon would be in the air, they should have just taken off. It was a 12 hour flight to Singapore, unlikely that he'd be monitoring his email account mid-flight, but I couldn't take any chances.

After what seemed an interminable amount of time an email dropped into his inbox from Peter Parker.

"Hi Simon, all ready for completion on 3rd. Just need you to transfer the remaining £800,000 purchase price. Have a great time in Singapore and remember to bring back those diamonds I asked you to get. Best Peter"

It was easy to copy the whole email together with the company logo and delete the original. Heart racing, I opened up my email server and using my spoof email account, I pasted the contents of Peter's email with one small addition.

"Hi Simon, all ready for completion on 3rd. Just need you to transfer the remaining £800,000 purchase price. Have a great time in Singapore and remember to bring back those diamonds I asked you to get.

Nearly forgot, send funds to my PP Client Account. Same sort code, account number 13496875.

Best Peter"

Hitting send, I breathed a sigh of relief. So, Parker was in on the smuggling too, although I didn't care. All I wanted was for Simon to land in Singapore, check into his hotel and transfer the funds to the PP Client Account, which was, of course, mine.

To pass time, I retrieved the stash of black bin bags I'd bought and gleefully bagged up the rest of Simon's clothes, ready to take them to a charity shop. They could have his Saville Row suits and tailor-made shirts. Cases were dragged out of the loft and packed with my own clothes and personal items.

A locksmith was called out to change the locks and finally I phoned my new solicitor. The charity I'd sold the house to was delighted to buy it fully furnished so they could use it as a women's refuge from day one. Completion was set for tomorrow, along with the purchase of my new home in Yorkshire. It seemed like a good time to phone Daniel, my yoga teacher.

"Hi sweetheart, are you up for a one to one yoga session this afternoon?" I smiled, thinking about the usual ending to our one to one sessions. Daniel. He was kind, loving, and oh so flexible and strong. We'd made love in positions I hadn't thought would be possible. And the orgasms. I felt a dampness begin as I thought about making love to him later.

Daniel had been all too willing to help when I'd said I needed to shelter some company profits for a few days, until after the end of the tax year. He'd given me his bank details, ready for me to make a transfer when I was ready. I'd also opened a new company PP Properties, and a bank account, ready for moving the money when it came in.

All I had to do now was trust that Simon wouldn't query the bank account he'd been asked to send the money to. That he'd make the deposit p.d.q. after he checked into his hotel in Singapore. Knowing that it could be another 12 hours at

21

least before the money was transferred, it seemed safe to leave the house and enjoy a therapeutic yoga session with Daniel. Several mind-blowing orgasms later I murmured against his ear, "it could be as much as £40,000 that I need to shelter. I may be moving the money later. Is that still okay with you?"

"For you Portia, anything" he'd declared, readying himself for more action. To be honest, I wasn't sure if I could keep this up long-term, but he was a means to an end. A beautiful sperm donor.

With a satisfied smile on my face I let myself back into the house later and checked my watch. "Give them a couple of hours to de-plane, get to the hotel and settle in. Time for some food, after all that exercise I'm starving." I thought.

My eyes began to get heavy as I browsed the net, checking for emails, checking the bank account. I know I dozed a while until around 1 in the morning I checked the bank account again. There it was in my PP Client account! £800,000. I hastily transferred £40,000 to Daniel's account and the rest to my PP Properties account. At last I could sleep for a while.

I was up early, eager for the day. Even the text from Daniel telling me he was keeping the money to start his own yoga studio didn't bother me. I'd half expected it. He'd earned the money and fulfilled his purpose, the pee stick showed I was pregnant. I hugged myself, at last I was going to be a mother.

My solicitor emailed me at 12. "All complete on sale and purchase. Please drop off keys for handover. Arrange to collect keys for new house from agents."

Logging in to Simon's email account for the last time left me laughing as I saw the string of emails between him and Peter Parker.

"Where's the money?"

"I've sent it to your client account as you asked."

"What are you talking about?"

"You asked me to send to your client account. I've forwarded the email to you."

"You total dickhead, the email wasn't from me! We've been spammed."

I couldn't resist it and typed a two word email to both of them.

"April Fool".

A Suspension of Judgement

She'd gone to bed early. To be honest she was a bit bored of her own company. There was nothing riveting on the TV and if she were completely honest with herself, which she rarely was, she was missing Steve.

She'd fallen asleep quite quickly, grateful at least for the absence of snoring from Steve.

She wasn't sure if she'd heard a movement or felt a movement. She'd lain very still, eyes closed, straining her ears for any sound. She was sure she'd locked up carefully before going to bed. All the security locks were on and the alarm set. There couldn't be an intruder, could there?

There was no noise, so she rolled over, luxuriating in having the big bed all to herself for once, when she felt someone sit on the bed. Her heart rate went up as she tensed, waiting, for what she didn't know.

"Hello Kate. It's alright, you can open your eyes. You're quite safe."

The voice was soft, reassuring and she opened one eye peering across the bed to see a shadowy figure seated where Steve usually slept.

"You can open both eyes, you might find it a little easier to see me" the voice continued "I'm here to have a chat with you."

Kate screamed and leapt out of bed, desperately searching for something she could use to defend herself against the intruder. She reached for her bedside lamp, thinking she would pull it free from the socket and hit the intruder.

"Don't put the light on" came the shadowy persons voice "you won't be able to see me at all in the light."

Kate rarely listened to anyone else, so as expected, she touched the base of the lamp to switch it on. Nothing. There was no-one there. She must have been hallucinating. She peered across the bed thinking that if there were someone there she would be able to see them.

Nothing.

"I must have been dreaming" she said to herself aloud "too many thriller novels."

"No, you weren't dreaming, I'm here, I'm real" the voice replied.

"Who the hell are you? Why can't I see you properly?" She still had her hand gripped round the base of the lamp, fully prepared to use it to defend herself.

"I'm your Higher Self Kate. I usually live in the dark shadows of your psyche, that's why you can't see me properly. Dim the light a little."

She touched the base of the lamp and sure enough she could make out a shadowy figure. She couldn't see it's features or even tell if it was male or female.

25

"I don't like you. Whoever or whatever you are go away."

The figure laughed. "Not just yet, we've got a lot to talk about. You're not very happy are you Kate and I'm here to help?"

"I don't need your help thank you very much. I'm fine. Just bugger off and leave me alone." Kate didn't swear very often, but she was desperately trying to cover up that she was actually quite frightened.

"It's okay to be frightened Kate, but I'm here to help you."

"I don't need your help thank you very much, I'm fine as I am."

If she'd been able to see it clearly, she would have seen the figure shrug it's shoulders. "Really Kate? You're fine as you are? Why do you think Steve left you at home this weekend?"

"It's a men only weekend, that's why." She retorted.

"Er, no. It's not. The other wives are having a great time while their husbands play golf. Massages, manicures, beauty treatments….. You could have been there too."

"Ugh. No thanks. What makes you think I'd want to spend the weekend with them? I'd rather be here on my own thank you very much."

Leaning toward her the figure whispered "Liar."

"How dare you. I don't like them. They're always on about their grandchildren, or their weight and how they should exercise more, the holidays they've just come back from or the shows they've been to see."

"You're very judgemental aren't you Kate? Did you know that when we judge others we see in them things that we don't like about ourselves, or things we wouldn't allow ourselves to do."

Kate sat up a little straighter, "I take care of myself, I exercise and I've never let myself get over weight, what's wrong with that?"

"Nothing at all Kate. It's when you criticise others that there's a problem. You see that puts a barrier between you and them. You're convinced that you're better than they are. Have you ever noticed that when you criticise it makes you feel superior or better about yourself?"

Kate was silent.

"Do you like yourself Kate?"

Silence.

"Well, come on let's be honest here. Do you like yourself Kate? Are you friendly, caring, compassionate? Let's play a game. Tell me 10 things you like about yourself."

"It's the middle of the night and I'm not in the mood for playing games" she snapped back.

"I forgot, you never are, are you? Humour me, the quicker we get this done for the night, the quicker you can go back to sleep."

"Oh fine, have it your way. I'm a good cook, I keep the house clean….. " her voice faded as she struggled to find things she liked about herself.

"Those are things you do Kate. Not really about you as a person. Are there things you don't like about yourself?"

"No." came the terse reply.

"Shall I tell you what other people don't like about you?"

Silence.

"I'll take that as a yes. You're critical of others."

"I speak my mind if that's what you mean" she retorted.

"You're critical of others" he repeated "you're very quick to find fault with things, you never give praise or compliments. Let me give you an example. Remember the last function you went to? The waitress was rushed off her feet trying to get everyone's meal to the table. What did you do?"

Silence.

"Let me remind you. You said something like "this waitress is hopeless, our food will be cold before we get it. Who decided to come here?" Double criticism, the waitress who was doing her best as was the person who organised the event. Did you stop to think how hurtful your comments were?"

Silence.

"I know you didn't, because you went on to criticise the man who drank too much, the singer with the band, the couple who couldn't dance very well, the woman wearing a low-cut dress. I could go on."

"I didn't say any of that" Kate protested.

"No, but you thought it, didn't you?"

Silence.

"You do that a lot don't you? You criticise people in your head. You do it to Steve but you never tell him what's wrong. How do you expect him to know what he's done that you don't like? He's not a mind reader."

"And I suppose you are then?" she retorted, getting quite impatient with the conversation. It was beginning to feel uncomfortable to have her critical habits exposed.

"Well of course I am. I'm your Super Ego, your Higher Self. I know exactly what's going on in your head. I wouldn't worry about it if it made you and the people around you happy. But it doesn't does it Kate?"

Silence.

"I'm going to take that as affirmative. I know you're tired so I'm going to let you go back to sleep." As she heaved a sigh of relief he continued "I want you to think about all the times you've been critical recently. What's it telling you? What don't you like about yourself? What wouldn't you allow yourself to do? And," he paused for effect, "what could you do differently in future?"

She didn't reply and as it began to disappear she could see the figure wave. "See you tomorrow".

It took Kate quite a while to get back to sleep. It had been disturbing to be the object of criticism herself, at least that's how she viewed it.

The next day she felt a bit bleary eyed. She made herself some breakfast and sat with a cup of coffee as usual, but it seemed tasteless. She thought about what the figure had said. Why was she so critical of others?

Her mind drifted back to her childhood. She'd lost count of the number of times her mother had criticised her. Whatever she'd done it wasn't good enough. How many times had she heard the mantra "money doesn't grow on trees" in response to a request for a new dress or shoes. As for school trips, she knew not to even bother asking if she could go. "We're not made of money you know."

Her coffee was going cold as she remembered the past. No wonder she'd felt inferior to her school friends, unloved by her parents. A cold, hard truth began to dawn on her. She still felt inferior to others, unloveable. Criticising other people created the pretence that she didn't like them anyway and that she was somehow better than them.

It was at this moment of revelation that the doorbell rang. "Who the hell is that" she thought. Peering through the net curtains she saw the woman who had recently moved in next door. "Oh god, it's the single mum with her 2 kids, what does she want?" They'd never actually spoken but Karen had decided that as there was no man to be seen, she must be a feckless single mother.

The doorbell rang again. Reluctantly, Kate went to the door and opened it.

The woman looked distressed. "I'm sorry to disturb you, I know we haven't properly met yet. I'm Sarah, I moved in next door a few weeks ago."

"Yes, I know who you are. What do you want?" asked Kate coldly, not being quite ready to let go of her critical ways.

"My mum has had an accident this morning and I need to go to the hospital. I don't want to take the children" she gestured to 2 small children who were clinging to her legs, "my husband isn't going to get back home for another week and I've no-one else I can ask. Would you mind very much watching them for me for a couple of hours? Please."

It was on the tip of Kate's tongue to refuse, but then she realised she had an opportunity to make up for judging Sarah.

"Okay, would it be best if I came to your house as they'll have their toys to play with. I'm sorry, I don't have any here, my kids are adult now and they don't have children of their own yet." She realised she was gabbling, making excuses, because for some reason she felt inadequate.

"That would be great, if you don't mind. I'm so grateful. This is Sam he's 6 and Charlotte, she's 8."

"Hello Sam and Charlotte, I'm Kate. Let me just get my mobile and keys and I'll come with you."

"They're good kids, they miss their Daddy and I struggle with them sometimes, but I'm sure they'll be good for you."

The little family, plus Kate made their way next door and Sarah quickly left. Kate looked around the living room, instantly comparing it to her own. There were boxes as yet unpacked and toys littered the floor. She took a deep breath "it looks like you haven't quite settled into your new home yet. Do you want to play with your toys?"

Charlotte looked on the edge of tears. Kate knelt to her height. "It's okay, I'm sure your granny will be fine and mummy will be back soon. What shall we do?"

"We moved here so granny would be close and could help mummy while daddy is away. Now granny might die."

"No, no, no. I'm sure she'll be fine and back home soon."

Sam had been very quiet up till that point. "Mummy said daddy would be back home soon, but he hasn't come back yet. He's in Abby Dabby. It's very hot there. Mummy said it was too hot for us to go there while daddy was working, so we've had to stay at home."

"It's Abu Dhabi silly, and when he comes home he'll bring us nice presents. We skype him every week, but it's not the same" she said wistfully "I miss him."

Kate blinked her eyes rapidly. How she'd misjudged this little family.

"I have an idea. How would you like to make some cakes for your mummy and granny? Let's see what she has in the kitchen. Ah, I see she hasn't had time to clear up from breakfast yet. Shall we do that and then make cakes?"

The children reluctantly agreed to help clear the kitchen before telling Kate that their mummy didn't have anything to make cakes with.

"Okay, no problem. Let's go to my house and we'll make some there."

The next few hours passed quickly. Kate had forgotten how much fun it was to make cakes with children as they helped stir the mixture and decorate the cup cakes they made. She realised that she had actually enjoyed spending time with the children. The kitchen was a mess, but it didn't matter.

By the time Sarah came home, with a sore granny in tow who had an arm in plaster, Kate felt happier than she had in a long time.

"Thank you so much" said Sarah "I can't begin to tell you how grateful I am. You're so kind to have had the children make cakes with you. Would you like to join us for dinner later? It 's only a beef casserole but there'll be plenty for all of us."

Kate surprised herself by quickly agreeing to join them later "I just need to do a bit of tidying up in my kitchen" she said as she left, smiling as the children each gave her a big hug.

That night she was asleep when she became aware of the presence of the figure who had disturbed her the night before.

"You've had an interesting day Kate. What did you discover?"

"A lot. I realised that I learned to criticise from my mother. She was definitely a pro at it!" Kate laughed as she said it. "I also learned that I make judgements about people based on their appearance and put my own interpretation on it,"

"Excellent, you've made a great start in uncovering your subconscious behaviour patterns. Anything else?"

"I thought about what you said. I wouldn't let myself get overweight, have an untidy house, be a single mother. So, it makes me feel superior when I criticise those who do."

"And does that make you happy or feel loved?"

"No, it doesn't." She sighed.

"What about today? Looking after the children? Helping your neighbour?"

Kate's face lit up "that was fun, I enjoyed it. I found it easy to chat with Sarah and her mum. Usually I feel inadequate, like I've got nothing interesting to say."

"I wonder if that's because your self-confidence took a battering as a child? What was that expression your parents were so fond of "children should be seen and not heard." No wonder you feel that you don't have a voice, or anything interesting to say."

"Yes, that's exactly it. And I feel jealous of people I meet who are confident and can talk easily to others."

"So you pick fault, criticise, to bring them down to your level."

Kate was quiet for a long time. Tears began to roll down her cheeks.

"How do I change?" she asked tearfully.

"It's easier than you think. Just accept people for who they are. We all have behaviour quirks but the bottom line is we all want to be loved and accepted for who we are. Just try a suspension of judgement. Of yourself and others, you might be pleasantly surprised how happy that could make you." With that the figure faded away.

"A suspension of judgement. I like that" whispered Kate as she drifted back to sleep.

Ella

Chloe slammed the front door behind her and sank to the floor. Another disaster. She'd thought he could be "the one", he'd complimented her singing, made her laugh, but now she realized that his jokes had all been at the expense of other people.

At the jazz club tonight she'd been the butt of his jokes. He'd put her down all evening to his friends, made her sound like a popstar wannabe and, even more incredible, had the nerve to think he'd be sharing her bed at the end of the night. What a tosser, she thought.

With her favourite Ella Fitzgerald CD weaving its magic round the room, she poured herself a glass of wine and began to sing.

"Some day he'll come along the man I love, and he'll be big and strong, the man I love and when he comes my way I'll do my best to make him stay. Maybe I'll meet him Sunday, maybe Monday..... oh who am I kidding, who's gonna love me." She knocked back the glass of wine and dissolved into tears.

"My oh my, who's feeling sorry for themselves? Just because one man turned out to be a jerk, don't give up on 'em all."

Chloe bolted upright and looked for the source of the voice but she couldn't see anyone. She frantically rushed to the front door to check it was locked.

"Who's there? You'd better get out now, I'm calling the police." Her voice began to shake as she realized that she couldn't see her phone.

"Oh, I wouldn't do that honey, it's me Ella, just turn the lights a little lower and you'll see me."

"Ella? It can't be." Chloe whispered "I must be drunk, too much wine" as she cautiously turned the lights down.

"Oh god, I can see you, you're all hazy."

"Well what do you expect girl? I am dead you know. Now you and me are gonna have a little chat. First of all, why you shedding tears over that no good man?

"I thought he was the one, you know the one I love. But I realized tonight he doesn't really love me at all. He hates my taste in music. He was always putting me down. He says I can't sing….." her voice trailed off as she realized she was confiding in a ghost.

"Well, he clearly has no taste in music at all if he doesn't like my music." Ella rolled her ghostly eyes "your voice isn't bad, of course it's never gonna be as good as mine, but with a little training you could be real good. Now, I've got Freddie waiting for me, we're scatting some Queen songs, so I'll come back soon. You get yourself to sleep and stop crying over that no good man."

"Wait, don't go." Chloe called as the hazy form began to disappear. Too late, Ella had gone. Chloe shook her head trying to clear it. "Too much wine" she muttered, "far too much wine and an overactive imagination."

 The next morning was bright and cheerful, Chloe felt her spirits lift as she resolved to put the previous night behind her and start afresh. She went for a run, did some yoga and cleaned the flat thoroughly before showering. "Well what do I do now?" she thought as she surveyed her pristine surroundings "I guess I could do some singing practice."

Chloe put the Ella CD on to play and listened carefully to Ella's voice, her phrasing, tone and rhythm. Turning the volume down on the CD player, she began to sing, trying her best to sound like Ella. "It's no good, I'm never gonna be as good as her, I don't know why I'm bothering, I may as well sing Lady Gaga stuff."

"Lady Who?" came a familiar voice from the bedroom "in my day gaga meant you were foolish. Is the woman a bit crazy or what?"

Chloe peered into the dim bedroom and could just see a hazy shape sitting on the chair.

"Er, hello Ella. Lady Gaga is a pop star and she does do some crazy stuff, but people like her music." Chloe flopped onto the bed "if I'm going to make a living from singing, I've got to be better and sound more like you did."

"You know you're too hard on yourself. There ain't never gonna be another Ella Fitzgerald, so you may as well get used to it. But you've got a good voice, like I said, with some help you could be real good. You know I sang other people's songs, did my own versions, made them my own. Folks just happened to like them. Everyone does it. I'm flattered you want to sing my songs, but you gotta sing them your way, put your emotions into them. You gotta sing from your belly, not your throat, let your breath push the notes out easy like. Try scatting with some of the songs. I gotta go now, Freddie's waiting, you go try out what I just said and I'll catch up with you soon."

"Oh god, I really am losing the plot. Singing lessons from a ghost, and what the heck is scatting?"

Deciding she had nothing to lose, Chloe wandered back into the lounge and practiced singing from her belly, letting her throat relax. She sang several of her favourite Ella songs, then tried putting her own take on them, changing the notes and phrasing here and there.

After an hour or so, she felt quite pleased with her progress. Her throat was getting dry so it seemed like a good time to take a break and make herself a coffee. As the kettle was coming to the boil her front doorbell rang. She cautiously peered through the spyhole and recognized the man who lived upstairs. They'd passed each other a few times going in and out of the building but they'd never spoken.

She opened the door a few inches, "Have you come to complain about the noise? I'm sorry, I've been practicing all morning. I'll stop now."

"No, its fine, I'm not here to complain. I've enjoyed listening to you, I wondered if...., look it's a bit awkward having a conversation like this, may I come in?"

"Go on girl, let him in, this could be the one," a ghostly voice echoed through the flat "he likes my music, he must be okay."

Chloe looked over her shoulder "will you go away" she whispered urgently.

The man at the door held his hand up "sorry, I shouldn't have disturbed you, I'll go."

As he turned to walk away Chloe called "no, I didn't mean you, please, come in, I'm just making some coffee, would you like some? I'm Chloe." She realized she was gabbling and shut up as she stepped aside to let him in. He looked big and strong, tick. He was good looking, tick. He liked Ella Fitzgerald, tick, tick, tick.

They both began to speak at once.

"I'm Nick, I play at the jazz club."

"How do you like your coffee?"

As they drank their coffee, they discovered a mutual love of jazz, Ella, Jamie Cullum, Louis Armstrong.

"Have you tried scatting?" he asked.

"That's strange, Ella, I mean someone mentioned it earlier. I'm not familiar with it."

"It's where you do improvisations on a melody using meaningless words like be bop de doo dop instead of the words of the song. Ella was considered the best at scatting in her day. We could find some videos on YouTube if you like."

The next few hours flew by and they arranged to meet again the next day. "I run in the mornings, do you want to join me?" Chloe asked, delighted when Nick said he'd love to.

A few days later Ella dropped by "well child, I see you've been practicing. You're sounding real good you know. I like that Nick you're seeing, he's a man of good taste. Plays in a band at the jazz club. You gonna join his band?"

"I like him too Ella, we seem to have so much in common. But I don't know if I'm good enough to sing with his band."

"You listen to me now, if you don't believe in yourself and give yourself a little love, how d'you expect anyone else to? I've seen you checking yourself out in the mirror. Do you think Nick looks at himself in the mirror and thinks I'm not good looking enough for Chloe, I'm not big and strong enough for Chloe? No, course he don't, he's just waiting for the right time to ask you to sing with his band. He's gotta know you know you can do it. Do you understand me? He ain't got time to nursemaid you on stage, you've gotta just go out there and sing your heart out. If he asks, don't let me down now, d'you hear me?"

With these words ringing in her ears, Chloe opened the door to Nick.

"You look gorgeous today" he said gazing intently at her. Without another word he pulled her close and gently kissed her. In the distance they could hear Ella's voice singing "Some day he'll come along the man I love....."

"Sorry, I shouldn't have done that" Nick apologized, pulling away.

"Actually, I think you shouldn't stop" Chloe reached up and wrapped her arms round him, holding him tightly.

"I really came to ask if you'd like to try singing with my band at the jazz club. Would you do a few numbers with us? We could do Ella and some other stuff and maybe some scatting...."

His voice trailed away as he looked at her uncertainly.

"Too damn right I would. When do we start rehearsing? I've got a few songs in mind."

And so it was that a few nights later Chloe took centre stage and sang from her heart to Nick.

"How much do I love you?

I'll tell you no lie

How deep is the ocean?

How high is the sky?"

She could have sworn she could see, standing by the bar, Ella and Freddie applauding.

The Social Influencer

Shelley peered in the mirror and wrinkled her nose in disdain at her morning face. She wasn't chocolate box pretty, but when she applied her make-up her face was transformed. False eyelashes, pencilled eyebrows, lips plumped to perfection and cheekbones artfully sculpted with makeup. This transformation took at least an hour every morning and Ryan was not allowed to see her until she emerged from the bathroom, ready to face her public.

The fact was that no-one, not even her best friend, never mind her partner Ryan saw her naked face. It was all part of the image of perfection to be portrayed. Time had to be spent each day deciding which clothes to wear, making sure she gave the right exposure to all her sponsors. No-one else seemed to understand how hard it was to maintain this illusion of perfection which was vital to her role as a social influencer.

As usual, Ryan waited outside the bathroom door, iPhone in hand ready to start filming for the day.

"Morning Babe" she leaned in and gave Ryan an air kiss on the cheek, careful not to smudge her lipstick.

"Morning Gorgeous, are you ready?"

Shelley felt a twinge of annoyance, of course she was ready, if not she would still be in the bathroom.

Shelley was of medium height, slim, not skinny but with curves in the right places. Her short, pixie style haircut framed her face. She often wished she had long, thick hair, that she was a little taller, a little prettier and was yet to accept that she was perfect as she was.

She'd fallen into her career as a social influencer purely by chance. What had started as a fun way to share videos of her life with friends on Facebook had transferred to YouTube and she now had several thousand followers. When she'd got together with Ryan, the numbers had increased as people followed their blossoming romance. With the increasing numbers had come more money-making opportunities, sponsorships, freebies etc.

Shelley and Ryan now enjoyed a way of life that wouldn't be possible if they'd had jobs. She'd scraped through a meagre 4 G.C.S.E.s and had no career aspirations beyond working in Next to get a discount on clothes. Ryan was very keen on fitness and had entertained ideas of becoming a personal trainer until he realised that there was a certain amount of work and financial investment required in order to qualify.

The great thing was that with their increasing fame as social influencers, Shelley was given beautiful clothes to wear, Ryan had the services of a personal trainer and local restaurants gave them regular free meals, all in return for exposure and endorsements.

They'd discovered some nice pub restaurants where they had no hesitation in necking 3 course meals and bottles of wine. No more McDonalds for them. Shelley delighted in flaunting the numerous new dresses she was given by a local boutique and of course, gave each donor their due exposure on the blog. The highlight of her day was going through her crammed wardrobe for the benefit of her followers, deciding which was going to be the "outfit of the day."

A few weeks ago, they'd announced their engagement and thrown a huge party at a local pub (courtesy of the pub owner) and within days had the choice of 3 wedding planners to help them organise the big day. Life was pretty good.

Ryan patted Shelley's bottom and pulled her to him for a hug as she passed him on the way to the kitchen. She smacked his hands away.

"Don't, you'll spoil my makeup, Wanda's taking me to try on wedding dresses this morning."

Wanda had been carefully selected as the woman who best fitted with their image and would therefore, be fit to be seen on camera with them.

Shelley hastily ate a bacon butty, washing it down with a latte coffee. After re-applying her lipstick she air kissed Ryan and rushed out to Wanda who was waiting in her car.

"We're going to a privately owned bridal boutique, the owner has closed it to anyone else for the morning. Can't have any sneak previews of your dress can we? Now, tell me what you want me to film for you."

Shelley thought for a moment.

"I'm getting the dress free aren't I?" smiling, as Wanda nodded in confirmation "then a shot of the outside of the boutique and the owner. They're going to give me champagne aren't they?" Wanda nodded vigorously. "Then I think I should try on several dresses. You can film me doing a cat walk in them, and we'll delete the footage of the one I'm going to wear."

Wanda nodded again and accepted Shelley's iPhone from her. Shelley posed in the doorway of the shop, pointing to the signage above the window.

"I'm so excited, I'm going to choose my wedding dress this morning, come inside with me" she gushed, pushing open the door.

Shelley was greeted by a slim woman who looked to be a similar age to her Mum. She wore a chic black dress her blonde hair styled in a bob.

"Shelley, Wanda, welcome to my boutique, I'm Hazel. We're going to have a fun morning trying on dresses. Lets drink a toast to finding the perfect dress for you." Hazel handed each of the younger women a glass of champagne, well it was prosecco actually, but she didn't think they'd tell the difference.

"Now, lets have a look at you. About 5ft 6" and a size 14 aren't you?"

Shelley nearly choked on her prosecco.

"What do you mean? I'm a size 10 if you don't mind." She knew her clothes had been getting tighter, in fact she'd split the seam on one of the dresses she'd been given, but a size 14. Never. She swiftly turned to Wanda, "stop filming now, don't you dare film that."

46

Hazel recovered quickly, she'd had to deal with many brides in denial before.

"Let me bring a few dresses for you to try and see what you like."

Shelley grew more depressed as the morning went on, each dress made her look fat, she couldn't deny she had a podgy stomach and large bottom. She left the boutique without choosing a dress, horrified at her figure. She knew she couldn't be pregnant, so was it all the free meals that had made her put on weight?

She confided in Ryan later, wailing that she couldn't possibly wear a wedding dress in a size 14.

"Come to the gym with me, I'm sure the personal trainer could help you. We could ask for help with getting our diet right. I bet someone would offer their services for free."

If looks could kill, Ryan would have been dead on the spot. Shelley had a lifelong aversion to exercise and wasn't about to change now. Grabbing the iPhone from Ryan she did a quick piece to camera explaining that her Mum needed help getting in shape for the wedding and was too disabled to exercise.

"Let's see if we can get lipo-suction for free shall we."

There was no offer for lipo-suction, but a few days later Shelley did get an intriguing message.

"Weight digestion. Non-surgical procedure digests your fat leaving you slim and beautiful." Shelley discreetly messaged back and arranged to go to the clinic for a consultation.

Seated in front of the consultant she confessed that it was herself who needed help to get back into a size 10 for her wedding dress. It was humiliating to reveal that she had grown to a size 14 and was now struggling to wear all the beautiful clothes she'd been given. She'd even had to resort to wearing an oversize Tshirt and leggings for this appointment.

"I think our procedure will be perfect for you. You will come in for a couple of days. On the first day we'll apply a paste to your tummy and pop you in an incubator. We'll keep the paste moist and within hours we see plant like growth. The plant sends tendrils down through your skin and feeds off the fat below. Your fat is literally eaten and you leave as slim as you usually are."

"Am I awake for this? Do I see what's happening? I've never heard of it before. Are you sure it's safe?"

"It's a fairly new procedure that we're offering, but it has been tried and tested and is 100% safe. No surgery, no anaesthetic, no scars. When we can see the plant has digested your fat we simply peel it off your skin. You'll be sedated all the time, so you can have a nice rejuvenating rest."

"And you'll do this for free for me?"

"Of course, all we ask is that you give us some publicity."

Shelley was so excited she could hardly wait to tell Ryan when she got home.

"Really? Are you sure? It sounds a bit weird to me? How can a plant eat your fat?" He put his hands on her shoulders and stood back looking at her from head to toe. "You know you're lovely as you are, don't you? In fact, I like the new curvier you." He pulled her close to try and kiss her but she pushed him away, protesting that he didn't understand.

The atmosphere was tense for a few days as they went about their day, videoing and sharing their activities. Ryan seemed to spend more time at the gym and was uploading lots of footage of him with his personal trainer. Shelley noticed but decided not to say anything, she didn't want him to think she was jealous.

One morning over breakfast Ryan explained that he'd been discussing home workouts and healthy eating plans with his trainer, Amy. After half an hour of 'Amy says this' and 'Amy says that' Shelley was forming an intense dislike of Amy.

"She's offered to come over and help us get our diet working better and to teach you some Pilates and yoga to help you get back to a size 10. I think we could really make it work and inspire other people to be healthier and exercise. What do you think babe?"

And so began a new regime of healthy eating, exercise in the morning and walks in the countryside. Ryan began to take on a healthy glow, his skin looked good, his eyes were bright and he was developing a toned body. The followers loved what they were doing and numbers were increasing day by day.

Shelley hated it. She sneaked off to her best friends most days and binged on burgers, fries and takeaways. Her weight crept up but Ryan didn't seem to notice. Wanda did.

"This healthy diet stuff doesn't seem to be working for you. Are you sure you're going to fit into your wedding dress?"

The dress had been chosen weeks previously and much to the annoyance of Hazel, Shelley had insisted on having a size 10. There wasn't a hope in hell that she was going to fit into it without some drastic action.

In desperation Shelley booked herself into the Weight Digestion clinic for the next day. There was no time to lose.

She was reassured by the hospital like appearance of the place and was taken to a room with what appeared to be an oversized incubator.

"Just put on these paper knickers and the gown and settle yourself down on the bed. We'll apply the paste and then put the incubator over you. I'm going to give you an injection to sedate you, so just relax. All the fat will be gone when you wake up."

The doctor applied the paste all over Shelley's tummy.

"The plant's going to have a feast on this lot" he murmured to his assistant.

Over the next few hours the plant germinated and tiny roots pierced the skin sucking up the fat from Shelley's tummy. The plant quickly grew to around 3inches high and tiny yellow flowers appeared.

"I've not seen that before, looks pretty." Thought the assistant who was charged with monitoring Shelley. It had been a tiring day and before long her eyes were heavy and she was dozing off in the chair. She woke with a start several hours later and peered at the incubator.

Screaming, she rushed out to find the doctor.

"The plant, it's spread, it's all round her bottom and down her thighs, it's at least 6 inches high and covered with yellow flowers. We need to get it off."

A frantic hour followed as the incubator was removed and the plant pried away from Shelley's skin. It was firmly stuck in places and needed to be scraped away leaving the skin red.

"That was close, but look, the fat's gone. Let's leave her to rest a bit longer and then we'll bring her round."

Shelley went home that night, beaming as she anticipated Ryan's reaction to her new slim figure. But he wasn't there. Instead a note on her pillow informed her that he'd left. He was tired of her being totally self-centred and her lack of support for the new direction he'd taken with their blog.

I know you've been sneaking out and eating rubbish. I can't take that you've lied to me. I'm calling off the wedding and setting up a new blog with Amy. I've taken my clothes, so I won't need to come back.

Shelley was distraught. She cried the entire night. What would her followers think? She and Ryan were a brand. What would happen to the sponsors, all the free clothes and meals. What would she do? She'd have to pretend that she'd called off the wedding, she couldn't possibly admit to being dumped.

She made her way to the bathroom, showered and spent an hour repairing the ravages of a night spent crying. Slipping easily into a size 10 dress didn't cheer her up.

She was so wrapped up in her misery that she never even noticed the green shoots with tiny yellow flowers growing out of her navel.

Space on the Menu

After three weeks in Bahrain and with at least another to go, Dina was tired, very tired.

The hotel was luxurious, the job was going well, she'd be finished on schedule, but she was tired of eating on her own every night and climbing into a huge lonely bed.

She'd been amused to realise that the waiters in the restaurant had mistaken her for a high-class prostitute, cruising the hotel restaurant and bar for a customer. They'd been polite, but cool. Once they'd got it that she was in Bahrain working on an important project their attitude had swiftly changed. Instead of being shunted into a corner table, she was given a table of her own on a raised dais at the side of the dining room where she could people watch whilst she ate her solitary dinner.

This particular evening Dina looked forward to a quiet meal and an early night. She'd talked to her husband, Frank, earlier, catching him before he headed off to bed. She'd pictured him sitting in their living room, gazing out at the rain filled skies, whilst she had looked out on yet another stunning sunset over the city. It had been reassuring to know that he was missing her, just as much as she missed him.

Walking into the restaurant she was surprised to see a man sitting at 'her' table. Sighing, she was relieved to see that the table next to him was vacant and swiftly made her way there.

The man exchanged brief smiles with her as they placed their orders with the waiter.

"Hi, are you on your own too?" he asked as they sipped their drinks, waiting for their starters.

"Yes, I've been here 3 weeks but I expect to be finished in a week then I can go home."

"Where's home, do you mind if I ask?"

"England, I live on the South Coast. I'm here installing a computer system for my company."

He looked impressed.

"I'm from the States, guess my accent gives that away. I'm here selling Boeing engines to the Arabs. To tell the truth, I should have been at a reception tonight, but I just couldn't face going. I miss my family and I'm ready to go home. Do you have a family at home?"

Dina told him about her husband and her daughter who would be getting married in the near future. "I know what you mean, I miss my family too. Travel is good, I love my job but you miss out on so much. How many children do you have?"

They chatted a while and he told her about his wife and four sons whilst they ate their starters.

"I tried to keep them separate from my work, we didn't live on the base. I wanted them to have as normal a life as possible, given what I did. I used to love walking in the woods with them when they were younger." His voice trailed off.

"Look, I hate eating on my own, do you mind if I join you?"

Dina introduced herself as he moved across to her table. He seemed like a nice enough man, perhaps a decade older than herself, medium height, pleasant face, when he smiled it revealed a gap between his two front teeth. He shook hands with her.

"Nice to meet you Dina. I'm Pete. Do you work away from home a lot?"

"Yes, I've worked in a few places round the world. I get looked after well, but it's funny you never really get used to it. How about you? Does your work take you round the world too?"

"In a manner of speaking. It certainly used to. Not so much now."

He leaned back in his chair and gave her a quizzical look.

"You're a very unusual woman Dina."

Dina's heart sank. He'd seemed like a really nice family man, was he about to come on to her? How was she going to make an exit without having her main course? Before she could say anything, he continued "most people ask me about the moon."

"The moon?" she echoed, perplexed.

"You don't know who I am do you?" he asked with a grin. She shook her head. "I'm Pete Conrad, I was the third man to walk on the moon. Apollo 12. That's all most people want to talk to me about. It's kinda why I didn't want to go to the reception tonight. I find myself saying the same thing over and over. No, it's not really soft and queasy. Yes, I did say 'Whoopie! Man, that may have been a small one for Neil, but that's a long one for me' for a bet."

Seeing her raised eyebrows he continued, "An Italian reporter was convinced that Neil was told what to say when he stepped on to the moon. When he said 'one small step for a man' he was referring to the step down from the lunar module. Neil's a lot taller than me, it was a small step for him. I told this reporter what I would say when I stepped down from the module." He shook his head and grinned "she never did pay me."

Dina in turn leaned back in her chair as she studied the man sitting across from her. She would never have guessed by his appearance or his manner that he was a world-famous astronaut.

"I can't begin to imagine what it must have been like."

"It's incredible. I'd been up on the Gemini programme before Apollo 12. We beat the Russians record for space endurance by 3 days and set the record for the highest orbit of the earth. That was something else. Looking down at the earth from 853 miles high. It was like looking at the globe you see in your classroom. I remember saying to Houston they could relax, the world really was round. I got letters from the Flat Earth Society telling me I didn't know what I was talking about!" He laughed as he recounted the anecdote.

"It sounds amazing" murmured Dina, fascinated and not wanting to interrupt.

"Yep. Apollo 12 was interesting. The flight was extremely normal for the first 36 seconds, then after that it got very interesting. We got hit by lightning twice, blew some circuits. I told Houston that perhaps we should do more all-weather testing! Anyhow they talked us through fixing the circuits and we went to the moon." His gaze seemed to be focused faraway as he quietly continued "it's incredible, almost impossible to describe. You see the earth getting smaller and the moon getting bigger. The stars getting bigger and brighter. The Milky Way, so bright and so very beautiful."

"It was a blast, I was there with two of my navy pals. We had a lot more wriggle room than Neil had as I'm much smaller." He was quiet for a moment before he continued with a wistful tone in his voice. "When you're up there, it's hard to describe, you realise there's something so much bigger than all of us down here. It makes you wonder why we can't all be a lot nicer to each other. It's difficult to find anything else that challenges you after walking on the moon. One of us got God, another found the bottle."

"And you? What did you do?"

"Oh I went up to the Skylab, there was a bit of a problem there so we did a couple of walks and got it fixed."

Dina was astonished, he said it as if it was nothing more than fixing up his car or motorbike.

"Spacewalks?"

"Yeah. I ride my motorbikes now. I love riding fast, it's exhilarating and gives me a kick. Not quite as exhilarating as going up in a space rocket, but hey, life on earth's pretty good."

The rest of the evening passed by quickly and Dina wished Pete goodnight. Her head was full of their conversation. When she got back to her room she couldn't wait to tell Frank and picked up the phone to call him.

"Are you okay? What's wrong? Why are you calling?" he asked her drowsily as he looked at the alarm clock.

"Frank, you'll never guess who I just had dinner with."

"I don't bloody care who you had dinner with" came the swift reply "it's 4 o clock in the morning. Bugger off and let me get back to sleep."

Dina never saw Pete Conrad again, and tucked the memory of her dinner with him away in the back of her mind.

She was reminded of it some 15 years later as she was scanning through the news headlines "Third man to walk on the moon dies in motorbike accident." "Look Frank," she showed him the newspaper "it's the astronaut I had dinner with remember, when I was in Bahrain, he's died."

Although they'd only been strangers who had shared one evening together, she'd never forgotten him and how he wished we could all be nicer to each other. Dina remembered how he'd talked of something so much bigger than all of us and she wondered if he was somewhere high above the earth, looking down, maybe thinking 'This is familiar, I've been   up   here   before.'

The Smile

Maybe you know that feeling. You're half asleep still and there's a memory hovering at the back of your mind. And then suddenly it emerges in full colour and it's as if you're living it again. You can't help it, you smile.

It was like that for him that morning. Drifting into wakefulness he remembered the night before. The soft arms wrapped around his neck, the wetness of the kiss on his cheek. The way she had smelled. Her voice telling him she loved him. And there it was, the smile.

He hadn't got around to opening his eyes when he heard his wife's voice. "Hi there sleepy head, good morning. You were late to bed last night. Are you okay? What are you smiling about?"

"Hi there yourself gorgeous. How are you today?" he ruffled her hair and drew her close to him. As she snuggled her head on his shoulder, he kissed her. He felt very pleased with himself. He smiled, content, all was well in his world.

She wondered what he'd been smiling at. Raising her head she could see he was still smiling.

"What is it?" he asked.

"Nothing, I just wondered why you were smiling."

"Why wouldn't I smile when I'm waking up next to you" he answered, pulling her back down into his embrace.

She didn't worry that he hadn't answered her question. She knew that he liked to keep some of his thoughts and feelings to himself. He worked hard, often long hours, building his business and he'd said many times that he didn't want to worry her with trivia or things she could do nothing about.

Sometimes she wished he would share more with her. Sometimes she felt like he shut her out, held something of his feelings back from her. She knew his parents had never been particularly demonstrative or affectionate so tried not to worry about it.

But this morning she really wanted to know what had made him smile. She knew from the little he did say that the business was steadily growing, but it still needed him to be very hands on.

"Come on, tell me. What were you smiling about when you woke up?"

"I don't know, I can't remember now. Forget it." Untangling himself from her he levered himself up and out of the bed. "I've got an important meeting today, I may have to take a client out to dinner, but I'll try not to be too late home." He kissed her again before heading off to the bathroom to shower and dress.

She lay there a little longer before she too got up, getting ready for the day. "He did seem very happy this morning" she mused "I've not seen him smiling so much for a while." She shrugged her shoulders and left the bedroom.

Perhaps you've had that feeling too. There's something going on, something a little different to usual. But you can't quite put your finger on it.

The smile lingered all day. Each time he re-lived the memory of the night before he felt his heart swell in his chest.

He smiled at everyone he saw that day and they smiled back at him. He was reminded of the poem by Spike Milligan.

He couldn't wait for the evening to come.

His meeting and client dinner had gone well, he'd got the deal he wanted. It was very late when he got home. His wife had gone to bed.

He crept up the stairs, his smile wide with anticipation. And there it was again. The soft arms wrapped around his neck, the wet kiss on his cheek. That distinct fragrance of her.

"I love you Daddy" she whispered sleepily as he tucked her back into bed.

Spike Milligan – The Smile

Smiling is infectious,

You catch it like the flu,

When someone smiled at me today, I started smiling too.

I passed around the corner

And someone saw my grin.

When he smiled I realized

I'd passed it on to him.

I thought about that smile,

Then I realized its worth.

A single smile, just like mine

Could travel round the earth.

So, if you feel a smile begin,

Don't leave it undetected.

Let's start an epidemic quick,

And get the world infected!

Sunset, Sunrise

The sun had just set as he slipped away. She'd been holding his hand, lost in her own thoughts, wondering when he would go. She'd been gazing out to the horizon watching the sun dipping ever lower in the sky, painting the clouds with touches of pink and gold. It was as the sky turned from gold to orange to deep crimson that she felt the grip on her hand loosen. He was gone.

"Yes, yes, I know. You'll be back on Friday and I have to make sure your dinner suit is ready. Yes, I know I'm cooking dinner on Saturday for 8 of us. Do you want me to email the menu for approval?" She couldn't resist the hint of sarcasm, though she knew if he picked up on it she would regret it. But he'd been too busy stowing his bag and briefcase in the back of the Jag. "Got to go, I've got a long way to go and I can't afford to be late." With a perfunctory peck on her cheek he was gone.

"Tenerife, that's where I'll go." She'd heard so much about Tenerife, the beaches, mountains, sunshine, the friendly people. She'd been learning Spanish in her spare time and was reasonably confident that she could manage a basic conversation. "Oh, to get away from the winter and the long dark nights."

She'd been 20 when they met. Her home life had been hazardous to say the least, living with parents who both had a short fuse on their tempers. She learned very early on to make herself scarce when an argument erupted and to never, ever answer back. He'd seemed like a knight in shining

63

armour coming to rescue her. How she'd longed to be loved. It had seemed to be the perfect marriage. To everyone else. Not to her.

"What did you think of the meal tonight love? Do you think your guests enjoyed it?" she asked, desperate for some hint of positive feedback from him. "What? Why are you asking? They cleared their plates didn't they?" The look he gave her was scornful. She was used to it, but it still hurt. Trying again she asked "did you get the deal wrapped up? Did it go okay?" The men had disappeared to his study whilst she did her best to entertain the wives.

Her thoughts drifted to Tenerife. "Perhaps I could get a late deal. I'll look online." There was enough money in the bank for her to go wherever she wanted. She'd start with Tenerife and maybe get more adventurous later.

It had been two years since the cancer scare. A routine check up at the doctors had revealed some abnormal cells and she'd had a colposcopy. She'd been sick with worry waiting for the results but it had come back clear. She hadn't told her mother, only her best friend. He hadn't been interested. "You'll be fine" he'd said when she asked him to go to the hospital with her. She still remembered the argument when she'd explained that she wouldn't be well enough to drive after the procedure. In the end her friend had taken her.

Why was she such a doormat? She was furious with herself. After ten years of a lonely marriage it was obvious that he would never really love her for who she was. He scoffed when she wanted to do teacher training saying her job was to look after him. He was tolerant when she went out to yoga, though she'd had to lie and say the teacher was a woman. It would not have gone down well if she'd told him the teacher was a fit young man. She couldn't understand his jealousy, she'd not done anything to provoke it.

Tenerife was lovely. Just what she'd needed after the previous few months. Determined to put them behind her she walked along the promenade pausing to watch the beach volleyball players in Los Cristianos. The waiter at "her" restaurant greeted her. "Good morning Senorita, Buenos Dias. What can I get for you today?" She smiled at his greeting. He knew full well that she was a Senora, not a Senorita but it still made her feel good. Each day she felt a little younger as if her cares were lifting off her shoulders. Every morning she'd rolled out her yoga mat and done her sun salutations. She'd been up extra early that morning. The sky had still been dark, the moon and stars visible. "Moon salutations" she'd thought as she stretched her body into upward dog and downward dog.

It shouldn't have surprised her really. They barely had sex once a month. She was on the pill as he'd made it clear he didn't want her getting pregnant. But there it was, he'd been cheating on her. Why else did he have a condom in his trouser pocket? She wondered if he'd left it there deliberately when he'd told her to take the suit to be dry cleaned. He must have known she would empty the pockets. She'd confronted him and he'd tried to bluff his way out of it. "It's not mine, I found it in the hotel bathroom and put it in my pocket."

"Really? What kind of fool do you take me for?" Suddenly all the nights away from home "working", the late evenings at the office made sense. The frequent phone calls from his secretary, the way he shut his study door when she called. "It's her isn't it? Your secretary."

"Yes, it is" he'd exploded "what made you think I'd be faithful to you? For God's sake woman, you're pathetic. All you do is keep house, cook and go and do your silly yoga stuff. Did you think I didn't know the teacher is a man? I had him checked out. Have you been doing some extra positions with him? I know all about these men, they only run classes so they can prey on women like you. Pathetic woman."

She'd stepped away from him, stunned by the vitriol he was spewing. She felt sick. He'd been spying on her and said nothing. What a fool she'd been to think he wouldn't.

"You needn't think you're going to divorce me. You'll get nothing. I'll make sure of that. You'll get exactly half of nothing." She'd covered her ears and run from the room.

At dinner that evening she noticed a man about her own age sitting at the next table. He was alone, like her. He looked up and smiled and went back to eating his meal. Out of the corner of her eye she looked at him. Blonde hair, blue eyes. Warm smile. He looked to be a little taller than her and slim. She returned her attention to her own meal until she heard the man chatting in Spanish to the waiter. She wondered if he lived on the island, but he was as pale skinned as she was.

The solicitor she'd been to see had been very kind. "He's a bit of a bully isn't he, but he will have to pay you, there's no question of that. Sit tight, whatever you do don't leave the marital home and we'll serve the divorce papers on him. If he gets abusive keep a diary of whatever happens and if you feel in any way threatened or in danger call the police."

He'd been apoplectic when she told him she was filing for divorce. "You can't, I won't let you." She'd kept a diary as instructed and lost count of the number of times she had called the police when he became threatening or abusive. He was clever. He never physically attacked her. It was a constant stream of vitriol, "breaking" her things, hiding her jewellery, slashing her clothes. She moved into the spare room and had a lock put on the door. He kicked the door down.

After dinner she wandered out onto the terrace and chose a seat where she could watch the sunset. It was her favourite place to sit. Peaceful, where she would not be disturbed. She sipped her sangria, wondering if she would see her fellow diner again. He'd seemed like a nice man, smiling and laughing as he'd chatted to the waiter.

The last argument had been awful. He'd been drinking whisky all evening and she'd tried to stay out of his way. "You're still my wife, I'm still paying for you to live here so you can damn well share my bed tonight" he'd snarled, gripping her wrist tightly as she tried to get away. He was bigger than her, heavy and thickset. As she struggled with him, his face turning redder and redder she wondered what she had ever seen in him. He let go her wrist suddenly and she fell to the floor, hitting her head. He clutched his chest his face contorting in pain. She was suddenly scared as he collapsed and fell heavily on top of her. She could barely breathe. The weight of his body was crushing her.

"No, no, no. Let it go." She thought, taking a large gulp of her sangria. "It's over, over, over. Why had she thought of it again, would she ever be free of the memories?"

"Are you okay? You looked a bit distressed then. Do you mind if I join you?" It was the man from dinner.

"Oh, no. I mean yes. Sorry, I'm not making a lot of sense am I? I don't mind if you join me, I just got a bit lost in a bad memory and I'd be grateful for the company."

"I'm not surprised you sit here, it's a great view of the sunset isn't it? Hi, I'm Mark by the way. I could use some company too."

They chatted for the next few hours as if they were old friends who had known each other for years. She felt more comfortable and at ease with a man than she could ever remember. She discovered he was a Spanish teacher and came to Tenerife as often as he could. "I wish I could claim it as a legitimate expense to keep my Spanish skills up to scratch" he'd joked.

"Are you here on your own? A beautiful woman like you? No husband? I've noticed you doing yoga and walking on your own."

"No, no husband not anymore. He died." She'd felt dazed from hitting her head and his body seemed to be pressing more heavily down on her. She couldn't hear him breathing any more. She wondered if she should tell him that as she'd lain underneath her husband, she'd debated with herself whether or not to call an ambulance. In the end her conscience kicked in and she'd struggled to heave his body off her and wriggle free. Too late.

"I'm sorry, I didn't mean to pry" he said, taking her hand in his.

"It's okay, really, it's okay. It wasn't a happy marriage. I feel like I've been set free, liberated, I'm happy for the first time in years."

Their attention was caught by the spectacle of the setting sun and the blaze of colours across the sky. The sun dipped lower and lower in the sky and still they sat, silent. She wondered if she'd scared him off by telling him that she felt liberated, freed by her husband's death. "Well, if I have it's too bad, I'm not going to lie any more to myself or anyone else."

She felt the grip on her hand loosen and he was gone. She sat still, waiting for the sadness to hit, but it didn't. "It was just a nice friendly chat, a pleasant evening." She thought, secretly hoping that she would see him again.

"I'm back. You were lost in thought and I didn't want to disturb you." He dangled a car key from his hand. "Come on, I want you to go change. Get some warm clothing, a jumper and a blanket from your room. There's something I want to show you."

A few minutes later he led her out to his car. He carried a bag with him. "Some extra clothes, blankets and refreshments

69

courtesy of the waiter. He didn't want the lovely senorita to be hungry or cold."

She looked at him quizzically. "Where are we going?" she asked.

"Mount Teide. It's the highest part of the island. The stars are spectacular and there's no moon tonight."

It took an hour to drive through the winding roads to the foot of Teide where they parked the car. He held her hand as he led her a little way from the car to where they could sit and stargaze. He was right. Away from all the light pollution the view of the stars was awe inspiring. They sat and chatted, drinking the wine and eating the food he'd brought. It was 3am before they returned to the car wrapping themselves in blankets and snuggling together on the back seat.

"I've set an alarm for daybreak, so try and get some sleep" he instructed as he wrapped an arm round her. With her head on his shoulder she felt as if she'd come home, she was exactly where she was supposed to be. She touched a soft kiss to his lips and he returned it.

They were woken by the sky and impending day break. Taking her hand, he led her to a vantage point where they could watch the sunrise. The sky was painted with gold, orange and vermillion as the sun began it's ascent.

"It's beautiful." she said.

"I never tire of coming here and watching the daybreak. It's like the whole world has been freshly painted with glorious colours. As if Nature's celebrating the start of a new day, a fresh chance to live life in techni-colour."

She smiled up at him. Her heart lifted at the idea of each day being a fresh chance to live. Reaching up to kiss him, she let go his hand. "I'll race you back to the car, loser buys breakfast."

The Siren

Esther glanced at the clock, Maisie had been gone a long time, she'd surely be back soon. Knowing her little sister, she'd probably been distracted by something or other. When they'd been young Esther had been like a second mother to Maisie. Despite the 11 year age gap, they were very close. She couldn't complain, the roles were reversed now as Maisie spent a lot of her time looking after Esther since Derek had died. Esther sighed, how she missed him. She'd go and put the kettle on, they could have a cuppa when Maisie returned. Then she remembered, Maisie had gone out to buy her a new kettle. It was the damnedest thing about being 80, she could remember her youth vividly, but ask her what she'd had for breakfast and she'd struggle to remember.

Maisie rushed into the house like a mini whirlwind.

"Hi Esther, I'm back and I've got your new kettle. Come and look. I found a retro design, it's just like the one you had when you and Derek got engaged, whatever happened to it?"

Maisie proudly lifted the kettle from its box and placed it on the counter.

"Ta da, isn't it just like the one you had?"

Esther clutched the counter and sank onto the kitchen stool. The years rolled back to 1957.

Esther had just got engaged to Derek. Her younger sisters Mary and Maisie had saved their pocket money for weeks to buy her an electric kettle. They proudly presented the box to her, eight year old Maisie scarcely containing her excitement. "Look Esther, it's going to play a tune when the water boils, can we hear it. Pleeease."

Esther carefully removed the kettle from the box. This was a thing of beauty, a far cry from the dented whistling kettle that sat on top of the stove. Dome shaped, in a shiny copper metallic finish and a curved black plastic handle, the kettle came with a lead to plug it into a socket. With her sisters looking on Esther filled the kettle with water and plugged it in. They all waited in anticipation for the water to boil.

Within a few minutes the kitchen was filled with the piercing sound of an air raid siren. Esther was frozen to the spot as their father rushed into the kitchen shouting "what the hell is that noise? Where's it coming from?" Her sisters were frightened. They'd never seen their father so wild looking, he looked deranged as he flung his arms out searching for the source of the sound.

"It's the kettle Daddy" Maisie whispered.

"Switch the damn thing off" he yelled clutching his head, pushing past Maisie as he ran out of the kitchen.

Mary hastily unplugged the kettle and emptied it. She hugged Maisie who was in tears as her beloved Daddy disappeared down the garden into his workshop. Esther meantime was transfixed. In her mind she had gone back to that awful time in November 1940 when she'd been just 6 years old.

The air raid sirens were wailing, a piercing sound that shattered the still night air. "Mummy, where's Daddy going? Why have we got to go in here? I don't like it, it's cold and dark. Why can't I sleep in my bed?"

Her father dropped to his knees to hold her tightly to him.

"Listen Esther, you and Mummy need to stay safe in the shelter. Be a good girl and try to sleep. I'll be back later." Over Esther's head he nodded to Doreen, "go to the shelter now, please. I need to know you're both safe. I don't know when I'll be back." With a quick hug and kiss he was gone.

Doreen took Esther's hand and led her to the Anderson shelter which had been built in the garden following the air raids which had started in August that year. Since then, many of their neighbours had packed tents and sleeping bags and left the city to camp out overnight in Abbey Fields in Kenilworth. Come the morning there would be a steady stream of people returning to the city.

The raids tailed off in October, people had breathed a sigh of relief, hoping the bombing was over. It was, until the night of 14th November when bombing had begun again. It seemed that the Luftwaffe were determined to wipe Coventry off the face of the earth this time. Incendiary bombs rained down and marker flares lit up the night sky.

"I'm frightened Mummy" cried Esther as the ground shook. The sirens screamed, the sound jangling every nerve in the body. The noise was so loud that even with her hands over her ears and head buried in her mother's lap, she was unable to block out the sound.

"We all are Esther, but we have to be brave. We're safe here. I'm with you and so are our neighbours, see we'll all be brave together."

"They won't be happy till they've flattened the city" snarled one man "I don't see the point of staying in here waiting to die." He pushed his way past the huddle of people crouching on the floor and stepped out of the door. They never saw him again.

Doreen made herself as comfortable as she could, cradling her daughter on her lap. She couldn't sleep. Every noise, every shudder of the ground as a bomb fell seared her nerves. She prayed all night that people were safe, that Esther's father was safe.

Esther supposed she must have slept. Someone pushed the door open a crack and they could see the cold light of dawn spread its fingers across the blackened, ruined city. It was eerily quiet.

"Mummy, I'm hungry. I need to go toilet." Esther whispered, fearful of making any noise.

"Shush, use the bucket in the corner. We must wait for Daddy to come home and tell us it's safe to come out, it won't be long now." Doreen hoped that she was right, that her husband would return and they could get out of this stinking hole in the ground soon. It felt like hours before the door to the shelter opened and there stood a figure she barely recognized. Esther hid behind her mother's skirts as her father stepped forward, his face anguished. He stumbled and clutched Doreen's shoulders.

"The cathedral. It's gone. Just the walls left. All the city centre. People are buried in their houses. We couldn't control the fires. There's bodies everywhere and," his voice broke "it's hell out there. I have to go back, do what I can. Stay in the house." With that he turned and retraced his footsteps toward the scene of devastation.

It was several days before Esther was allowed to venture out of the house. Each day her father went to the factory, working to get it running again. Each night he went out and returned, his face bleak, eyes sunken with exhaustion. She heard snatches of muted conversations between her parents. "No, it's gone. We don't know yet. Mass graves. Body parts everywhere." When her father snatched a few hours rest she could hear him sob in his sleep.

When they were finally allowed out of the house to get food Esther was horrified. Where a row of houses had stood there was only a deep crater and a pile of rubble. "Where's Aunty Sybils house gone, where are my friends?" Esther asked her father, gripping his hand tightly.

Her father's face hardened. "They're dead Esther. The bombs killed them."

The town centre was no better. Inside the cathedral which had stood for hundreds of years, there was just rubble. Only walls and the tower remained.

"Why did the Germans do this Daddy? Why?" cried Esther, tears streaming down her face. "To win the war" he replied grimly, "To win the war."

Back in 1957, Mary had hastily packed away the offending kettle.

"Esther, what's wrong? Why are you crying? Why is Daddy angry?" Maisie rushed over to her and held her tight. Wiping the tears away, Esther was grateful that Maisie would never have to go through the horrors of that November night.

"I'll go and see if Daddy wants a cup of tea, stay here" she said, gently disentangling herself from Maisie's arms.

Esther hurried down the garden path relieved that her little sister seemed alright. She heaved open the heavy workshop door to find her father slumped on a stool, head in hands.

"Daddy, do you want a cup of tea?" she stopped short as her father looked up, tears streaming down his face. Instinctively she rushed over and flung her arms around him. They clung together till the tears subsided.

"It's alright Daddy, it's gone now. We're safe."

The memories fading, Esther reached a shaking hand out to Maisie. "I'm sorry love, you'll have to take the kettle back."

The Gratitude Journal

Sam had refined the art of non-verbal communication, letting as many people as possible know that he was deeply unhappy. Doors slammed, monosyllabic answers, walking off when he was spoken to, deep and heavy sighs, a permanently pained expression. He made it very clear to everyone he came into contact with that life, in particular his own, was a bitch. In desperation his Mum had finally persuaded him to see the doctor, hoping that he had some sort of magic pill that would help cheer Sam up.

"Look, you're only 18 and you've had a bit of a tough time your Mum tells me. I don't want to prescribe anti-depressants so I'm going to suggest you come to our therapy group. It's for people like you, who are having a difficult time and it might help you. I'd like you to try that before we think about drugs."

Mum wasn't too happy, she wanted a quick fix and to get her son back, but Sam reluctantly agreed to go to the group.

The first meeting was the next evening in the doctor's waiting room. A circle of chairs had been set out and a youngish guy, wearing glasses was writing on a flip chart. Mum hovered anxiously by the door.

"Mum, go home. I'll see you later."

The young man put his pen down and approached Sam holding out his hand. He was casually dressed in a t-shirt and jeans and had a friendly smile.

"Hi, you must be Sam. I'm Paul and I'm leading the group. There's not many of us, take a seat wherever you like."

The seats gradually filled and Sam noticed there were people of all ages in the circle. Only one seat was left when an older woman rushed in and plonked herself down next to Sam.

"Hi, I'm Barbara. I haven't seen you before. Don't worry, you'll be alright."

Sam edged as far away from Barbara as he could. He didn't do talking to old people. He had nothing in common with them. Anyway, there didn't look much wrong with her, he idly wondered why she was in the group at all.

Waiting for Paul to begin, he looked around the room and it finally dawned on him that everyone else looked okay too. Why were they all there? They couldn't have real problems, not like him.

Paul began by asking everyone to give their name for the benefit of new members and invited them to share one thing from their gratitude journal if they wished.

There was a small flurry of activity as people retrieved notebooks of varying descriptions from beside their chairs. He couldn't help notice that Barbara had a neon pink notebook with a huge rainbow stuck to the front. He shook his head pityingly, old people.

As each person introduced themselves and read from their notebooks Sam began to feel angry.

"I'm grateful that it wasn't raining today and I went for a long walk in the woods."

Oh please, Sam thought, this was pointless.

"I'm grateful I slept well last night."

Sam couldn't remember the last time he'd slept well, his sleep was interrupted by nightmares about his abusive father.

"I'm grateful my friend came round to see me and gave me a hug."

Sam sank lower in his chair, he couldn't think of anything he felt grateful for. Zilch. Nada.

When it came to Barbara's turn, she winked at Sam.

"I'm grateful that today I knocked 15 seconds off my PB and cycled 5k in 10 minutes."

That made Sam sit up and stare. This woman didn't look like she could cycle 5k in 10 hours, never mind 10 minutes. She was a bit taller than his Mum, skinny, with grey hair cut into a bob. But an athlete? Sam didn't think so.

Paul led them through a guided relaxation, and Sam was surprised to find he was nodding off. The session wrapped up with the group being reminded to keep a daily gratitude journal.

"How was it Sam?" his Mum asked when he got home.

"Okay I suppose."

The next week Sam was a bit late, he'd been playing Call of Duty and lost track of time. The only seat left was next to Barbara. He groaned inwardly as he took his place. What would the old biddy say today?

"I'm grateful that my strength is improving, I did 20 press ups in 30 seconds today."

Ha, chance was a fine thing. Sam doubted if he could do 20 press ups, never mind Barbara. Those skinny arms surely couldn't do press ups. He began to wonder what she'd be grateful for next time. He couldn't understand why she was at the group at all, she seemed fine to him.

Again, he contributed nothing to the group. But when he got home he dug out an old notebook. He would never have admitted it to anyone, not even himself, but he was slightly intrigued by Barbara. He wondered if he too could do 20 press ups in 30 seconds.

He soon found out the answer was no.

Sam's fire and competitiveness had been crushed out of him by his bullying father. But somewhere deep within a little spark ignited.

He got his old bike out and cleaned it up. He even went for a short ride on it.

Each day he wrote one or two things, like 'today I went on my bike, I got to the next level on Call of Duty' but they seemed trivial things that didn't seem to help shift the deep well of misery within.

81

This went on for a few weeks and Sam felt he was no further forward than he was when the doctor suggested the group. He decided to give it one more week and then pack it in.

The session was different to usual. Nobody shared anything from their gratitude journals. Instead, Paul asked them to think about how many hours a day they spent online in Facebook groups, Instagram, Twitter, YouTube or gaming.

He then asked how many hours a day they spent with people face to face. How much time was spent with friends, family or neighbours?

Most people in the group spent several hours a day on-line and next to no time with people.

"The problem is that when you spend time in the virtual world, it cuts you off from the real world and all that it has to offer. This disconnection can make you feel isolated, uncared for and make depression worse. So, no gratitude journals this week, instead I want you to make an effort to talk to someone face to face every day."

There were a few horrified faces in the group, but Barbara jumped up.

"Come on everyone, lets start now and go to the pub and talk to each other. That'll be a good start."

The room quickly cleared, but Sam hung back. He was so not ready to be seen in public with this crowd. He nipped to the loo so they couldn't encourage him to join them.

When the room was clear he noticed that Barbara had left her gratitude journal on her chair. He quickly picked it up and hurried out but everyone had gone, including Paul.

'I can't leave it here someone might pinch it. Bugger, I'll have to take it home and give it back to her next week.' Reluctantly Sam stowed the journal in his bag with his own notebook and headed home.

In the privacy of his bedroom he took out Barbara's journal and opened it hoping to see an address where he could return the book. He didn't want to be the custodian of it for a week.

But no, on the front page in bold, red writing he read:

"Bloody Stupid Gratitude Journal"

What the fuck?

"What the hell have I got to be grateful for?"

Shocked and more than a little curious, he turned the page.

"What am I grateful for today? NOTHING."

"I wish I could drive, I'd run over the bastard who killed my family."

Page after page, the writing continued in this vein.

"Why should I feel grateful to be alive? Paul's a wanker. His family's alive."

"Bring back the fucking death penalty."

"Stupid moronic judge."

"I hope he gets beaten up and dies in prison."

Sam hastily tossed the book away from him. This was written by someone in a lot of pain. Surely not old Barbara who did bike rides and press ups? People like her didn't use language like this.

He realized that he'd had similar thoughts about his Dad after he'd beaten up Sam and his Mum the last time. He felt a simmering rage inside him beginning to bubble, burning to be expressed. Reaching for his own notebook he began to write, not consciously thinking about what he was writing, just letting his feelings pour out onto the page. By the time he finished he was shaking and tears flowed down his cheeks. The tears turned into raging sobs and suddenly, arms were around him, holding him close.

"It's alright Sam, we're safe now. He'll never hurt us again." They clung together until the tears subsided.

"I'm sorry Mum, I've been a pain in the arse, but I'll try harder."

"It's okay love, you've had a tough time, but now we need to heal."

The following week Sam went back to the group. He sat by Barbara and handed her journal back to her.

"I found it on your chair, after you left, I couldn't see you so I looked after it." He found he couldn't meet her eyes.

"Thank you Sam. I hope you read it. I had to hide for ages in the loo to make sure you had gone last week."

Sam's head jerked up in astonishment.

"You see, you have to let go of all the crap, the anger and hate so you can make space to let good stuff back into your life." She smiled sweetly at him "do you fancy going for a bike ride with me one day? Your mum could come too."

And to his surprise Sam said yes.

The Opal Ring

Evelyn sat on the bed looking around the cluttered bedroom, the wardrobe stuffed so full of clothes, the doors wouldn't shut. She sighed heavily. Her daughters, Lydia and Nancy, were right, there was no way she was going to get the contents of her three-bedroom house into the bungalow she was moving to. She'd best make a start before they arrived later. It was so hard, she'd lost her beloved husband Edward and now she had to let go of this house and all the memories it held. Where to start?

Evelyn glared at the dressing table next to her, the top strewn with hairbrushes and trinket boxes. Pulling open the top drawer she eyed the contents disdainfully. The drawer was crammed with greying bras and knickers which had all seen better days. Well, I suppose these can all go, I can treat myself to some new ones she thought, dumping the ancient undies unceremoniously in a pile on the floor. As she did, a battered ring box tumbled out of the mess and landed at her feet.

Evelyn stared at the box in horror, reluctantly opening it to reveal an opal ring. Her eyes filled with tears as she drifted back to memories she'd suppressed for years.

Her mother, slim and beautiful, with blue eyes and red-gold hair much as her own had been in her youth. Her father, barely remembered, just a photograph that showed him tall and handsome in his uniform before he went to war in 1914. Evelyn had only been five when her father left with his regiment and had no recollection of his leaving, the jaunty wave goodbye.

"It'll all be over in 3 months, don't worry we'll soon beat the Hun and I'll be back."

He had been back for a short while in 1916, a shadow of his former self. He'd been injured and sent home to recover. It seemed only a few weeks till he was considered fit to return to the front, leaving behind a tearful daughter and pregnant wife.

Through those awful years her mother, Margaret, had been strong, her belief in her husband unshakeable, sure he would return to her. They lived with Margaret's parents in their neat 3 bed semi. Grandmama and grandpapa were kind, but believed that children should be seen and not heard.

Evelyn had barely noticed the absence of her father. Her days were spent with Margaret, playing with her dolls or walking in the park. Occasionally, grandmama and grandpapa would walk with them and they would take bread to feed the ducks. Life was simple and she was blissfully unaware that the country was at war. At night she would sleep in a truckle bed in Margaret's childhood bedroom, delighted to share the room with her mother.

Evelyn adored her mother, the way she always had a smile on her lips and read her stories each night before she went to bed. She trotted along beside her in the park, bemused by the way Margaret's hair glinted red and gold in the sunlight, belly growing bigger as the pregnancy progressed, always wearing the opal ring.

"Your papa gave it me after you were born. He said the reds and golds in it reminded him of my hair. He had it made for me. One day it will be yours."

Sometimes Margaret allowed Evelyn to wear the ring as she played in dressing up clothes, wrapping Margaret's shawl round her, pretending that she was a beautiful lady like her mother. Vaguely aware that her papa was away fighting, it meant nothing to Evelyn, safe in her little world with her mama and grandparents.

Evelyn's little world came crashing down in November 1917. The day had started like any other till the knock on the door and the voice announcing a telegram for Mrs Margaret Smythe. She heard the scream first then her mother's anguished cry.

"No, no, not my George it can't be." The telegram fluttered to the floor like a leaf in the wind as Margaret dropped it from fingers suddenly nerveless. Clutching her throat, Margaret crumpled to the floor. Evelyn rushed to her mother's side and screamed for her grandparents.

"Grandmama, come quick. Mama has fallen."

The next few hours were a half-remembered blur. Whispered words. Killed at Passchendale. She's bleeding. It's not time yet. Get the doctor. Get the child out of the way. It's too early.

Grandmama had taken Evelyn by the hand leading her to her bedroom.

"Be good child and play with your dolls. Your mama needs you to be quiet. You may have a little brother or sister soon." With that Evelyn had been left alone, wondering what was happening to her mother but excited that the baby might soon arrive. She was terrified when she heard screams and tried to go to her mother, but she'd been locked in the room which suddenly felt like a prison.

It was many hours later that Grandmama had come and taken her by the hand. The doctor shook his head as they entered the room, dark in the gloomy afternoon light. A strange smell pervaded the air.

"Stillborn, I couldn't revive the baby. I'm not sure if the mother will live, she's lost a lot of blood."

Evelyn looked at the figure on the bed. This couldn't be her mother. This pale, lifeless creature, but yes, she had her mother's red-gold hair, wet now with sweat, spread over the pillows in a tangled mess.

"Mama" she'd rushed over to the bed and taken Margaret's hand. Her mother smiled weakly as tears rained down her face.

"Ssh, don't cry, I'll be alright. Be a good girl for Grandmama now. Give me a kiss my little angel."

Evelyn was taken back to her room and put to bed after a simple supper of bread and milk. She cried, not knowing what was happening to her beloved mother, before fatigue finally overcame her and she fell asleep clutching Margaret's shawl to her.

The next morning Grandmama had come into the bedroom and held her tightly. Stroking her hair, she told her that the baby and her Mama had gone to be with Papa in heaven.

"When are they coming back from heaven?" Evelyn asked, "will Mama be better when she comes home?"

Grandmama had cried, her face ravaged by grief.

"They aren't coming back Evelyn, we all have to be brave now and know that God is looking after them."

The following weeks were a blur. Evelyn's sole comfort was her mother's shawl which she wrapped around her and slept with. She could smell her mother's perfume clinging to the shawl, though the fragrance faded as the weeks went by. She left the only home she'd really known and was taken to live with her aunt. She missed her mother and grandparents dreadfully and couldn't understand the raised voices which hushed when she came in the room.

'There's no widow's pension, she's dead.'

'How are we expected to keep her?'

'We can barely manage now.'

'We could sell her jewellery, that might help.'

Everything had changed. No longer the adored little girl she was clearly unwanted, a nuisance. Sharing a bedroom with a cousin she hardly knew, given hand me downs to wear. Her aunt stern and forbidding, no affection shown to the orphaned child. No time for play anymore, Evelyn quickly learned to help with the chores, do as she was told and make

90

herself as invisible as possible. The opal ring had disappeared not to be seen again.

That is, until 1940.

Evelyn could barely wait to leave her aunt's house. In 1930 she began walking out with Edward and life improved dramatically. Edward lived in the next street and they'd gone to the same school, both leaving when they reached the grand age of 14. Edward had got an apprenticeship at a tool makers in Coventry and Evelyn, who was good with numbers, had been taken on at the Daimler factory in the accounts office.

By this time Evelyn had grown to be the image of her dead mother. Beautiful red-gold hair, blue eyes and a passion to escape from her aunt and be loved again. Edward knew all about Evelyn's past and spoiled her with gifts, nights out, little trinkets. She had no hesitation accepting his proposal of marriage and they wed in 1934 when they were both 25.

How wonderful it had been to set up home together. It was a two up, two down with an outside lavvie and tiny kitchen. Oh, but the bliss of being away from her aunt and with Edward more than compensated for any shortcomings in the house. She delighted in cooking for him, the intimacy of their nights and feeling loved again.

Edward suffered from asthma and needed an inhaler. They'd joined a cycling club, the doctor being convinced that the exercise was good for Edward's lungs. He still needed an inhaler, but managed very well, even on long trips to Wales for the weekend. Life was good, apart from the growing fears of another war.

'It's only been 20 years, surely the last war should have been the end of Germany?'

'It's that Hitler. Power hungry. He's invaded Poland.'

'What about Stalin and the Russians?'

'There can't be another war. Chamberlain will tell Hitler.'

Chamberlain did tell Hitler and the ultimatum was ignored. By the end of 1939 the country was at war again.

Production of the factories in Coventry was geared toward producing munitions and tanks. Men disappeared off the streets to join up and go to war. Evelyn was terrified that Edward would be called up. She was thankful when he was told he was in a reserved occupation, essential to the war effort. Besides, his asthma meant he was medically unfit to go to war and be killed. They both appreciated the irony, that having asthma might have saved his life.

Edward was determined to do his bit, even though he couldn't go and fight. He joined the Local Defence Volunteers and proudly wore his arm band proclaiming he was an LDV member. He would at times disappear for training in the use of munitions, blowing up the local quarry. They were woefully unarmed and he complained bitterly to Evelyn that most of the men had borrowed rifles, with little ammunition.

Despite this, life seemed to continue reasonably normally. By 1940 Evelyn was pregnant at last and they looked forward to the birth of their first child. She was still working at the Daimler when she walked home one chilly mid-November afternoon, clutching her coat and her mother's shawl round her. She walked slowly, by this time 6 months into her pregnancy and browsed in shop windows as she made her way home.

Evelyn never knew exactly why she stopped and looked in Gilbert the Jewellers shop window. There, in the middle of the window, with a spotlight shining on it was an opal ring. It had red-gold stones, just like her mother's.

With a rapidly beating heart, Evelyn pushed the shop door open and stepped inside. The bell above the door rang bringing the jeweller out of a small workshop at the back, where he had been polishing a necklace.

"Excuse me, you have an opal ring in the window, may I look at it please?"

The jeweller gave her a startled glance and brought a chair for her.

"Sit down my dear. I'll just get it for you. It's a cold day isn't it?" he reached into the window and brought the ring to her, placing it on a black velvet pad.

Evelyn's eyes filled with tears as she picked up the ring.

"It looks just like my mother's ring, I didn't know where it had gone. Can you tell me anything about it?"

It was getting late, nearly closing time but there were no other customers, so the old man picked the ring up.

"I made this ring in 1910 for a young gentleman." He put his loupe to his eye and examined it. "Yes, it is the one I made. It's hallmarked and dated 1910. I was very pleased with it, the little diamonds and the new art deco style of it. Some people say opals are unlucky, but I think they are lovely stones. I remember his wife had not long had their first child. He said the stones reminded him of his wife's hair, red-gold. Much like yours I imagine. I think that's why I remember it so well. I thought it was very romantic."

"How did it come back to you? Do you remember?"

The jeweller thought for a moment and fetched a dusty old ledger from the workshop at the back of the shop.

"I always make a record when I buy jewellery, who brought it in and what I paid for it. Just in case it was stolen."

He flicked the pages of the ledger as Evelyn watched him impatiently. He seemed to have bought a lot of jewellery from people. Page after page was turned as he went back through the years till he got to 1918.

"Ah, here it is. I bought it in August 1918 from a Mrs Canning. I don't know why, I put it in the back of the safe and forgot all about it till I decided I really should tidy up my stock. Not much call for jewellery at the moment with this war on."

He seemed not to notice that Evelyn had gone very pale, her hands shaking as she picked up the ring again.

"Mrs Canning was my aunt, she died a few months ago, cancer. She had no right to sell the ring, it was mine. My mother promised it to me. Please, will you put it back in your safe and don't sell it till I tell my husband about it. I'll tell him tonight and get him to come in and pay for it."

The jeweller looked shocked. He had heard some rum stories about jewellery, people down on their luck or being left something they didn't like. But this. Selling this young woman's ring. It wouldn't do at all.

"Of course, I'll tuck it in a box and put it back in the safe. Don't worry, you come back with your husband when you're ready. I'll try and do you a good price for it. You take care now, it won't be long till you have your baby will it?"

"It should be another 3 months yet, middle of February. Thank you so much."

Evelyn shook the jeweller's hand and exited into the dark evening, anxious to get home and tell Edward all about the ring.

She made sure she had given Edward his tea before she told him about the ring.

"It was my mother's I'm absolutely convinced. The jeweller, Mr Gilbert, said a Mrs Canning had sold it. That was my aunt. I must have it Edward, please will you buy it for me? It would be the only thing I have of hers, apart from this old shawl." She reached up and kissed him, only pulling away when they felt the baby kick him.

"See baby wants you to buy the ring for me."

Edward couldn't refuse her. He promised to go to Gilbert's jewellers with her and they would buy the ring.

"I've got to go now darling, I'm on duty tonight. Let's hope there's no more air raids. It's a bright night, perhaps that'll put them off. You go to bed and I'll see you later. Remember to get into the Anderson shelter if you hear the sirens." With a quick kiss, Edward left. She could see his breath misty in the air as he disappeared into the cold, dark night.

He hadn't been gone many hours when the air raid sirens sounded.

Oh, dear God, please keep Edward safe Evelyn thought as she quickly gathered up a flask of water, some fruit and a tilley lamp, carefully making her way to the Anderson shelter. She wrapped her mother's shawl tightly round her, hands clasped over her ears as the sound of bombs and incendiaries filled the air. She could hear screams each time the ground shook as a bomb fell. It sounded so very near, she was convinced the shelter would be hit any moment. Dear God, please keep Edward safe, please keep my baby safe, she muttered over and over, as the bombs rained down through the night.

Next morning, Edward's voice woke her as he banged on the shelter door. She emerged from the Anderson shelter into a strange world. The sky was filled with black smoke making it as dark as night, whilst the raging fires made it hot as a summer's day. They clung to each other, tears streaming down their faces.

"The town centre, it's all gone, the cathedral's gone. So many buildings on fire and people killed. Bodies everywhere." Edward clung to her, shaking with exhaustion, "it's like hell on earth out there, stay home Evelyn. I must go back soon." They looked up at their little house which had miraculously survived, whilst the houses on the other side of the road were nothing more than piles of rubble.

"Help the neighbours where you can, but stay at home, please Evelyn, it's too dangerous."

For the next few days Evelyn scarcely saw Edward as he joined the massive effort to find survivors and clear some of the wreckage of what had been their city centre.

He was working with a team of rescuers one day when he came across an old man standing on a pile of rubble, shaking his head, eyes filled with tears.

"Can I help you? Is there someone down there?" Edward shouted at the old man.

"No, no. That safe," he said pointing at a safe half buried in the rubble "it's all that's left of my shop, Gilbert's jewellers. It's got my stock in it. Can anyone help get it out?"

"We're really supposed to be searching for survivors, but give me a minute and I'll see what I can do."

It took a couple of hours shifting rubble until the safe was levered up, below was the broken body of a young woman with a child clutched to her chest. They stared, horrified.

"Nothing we can do for her now," whispered Mr Gilbert as he bent down, opened the door and scooped the safe contents into an old sack. "I must give you something to thank you."

"If you can find the opal ring my wife looked at the other day, I'd be happy to have that."

"The lady with the red-gold hair? Take it, maybe opals are unlucky after all."

Evelyn cried when she saw the ring, hastily tucking it into her apron pocket as Edward collapsed into her arms, coughing and wheezing.

Edward's asthma had got worse after that day. The doctor said it was all the dust, his lungs were damaged. Evelyn was convinced it was also due to the horror of what he saw in the aftermath of the blitz. He was never the same again, he wouldn't talk about the woman who'd been buried under the safe, the body parts he'd had to dig up. He was haunted by nightmares. Evelyn had put the opal ring away in her dresser, looking at it from time to time but never wore it.

Evelyn was brought back to the present by the sound of her daughters as they came into the house calling out to her. She snapped the ring box shut and threw it back into the pile of discarded undies.

"We'll be with you in a minute Mum, just making a cuppa. Do you want one before we get started?"

"Wow, you've made a start already. Let's get these picked up and put in a dustbin bag." "What's this Mum, there's a ring box here?"

Lydia picked up the box, "I remember this, it's an opal ring, it's lovely. You didn't mean to throw it away did you Mum?"

"Take it, I don't want it, the jeweller was right, opals are unlucky, I wish I'd never seen the damn thing again."

98

Exchanging knowing looks with Nancy, Lydia quietly picked up the box and put it in her pocket. "Okay, fine, lets crack on with sorting things out shall we?"

Lydia felt drained when she left Evelyn later. Her mother was a hoarder and she'd had a total meltdown when they'd tried to throw away an old shawl. She took the ring box from her pocket and slipped the ring on her finger, delighted that it fit perfectly. Crossing the road to where her car was parked, she wiggled her finger, entranced by the way the stones changed colour as they caught the late afternoon light.

She didn't see the speeding car until it was too late.

The Pencil Love Affair

It was Helena's first time at the writing group, she hadn't been sure what to expect and was relieved to have been warmly welcomed. There were seasoned writers and others, like herself, trying to get started. Details of a member's writing competition were passed around. As she skimmed through the information, a young woman around her own age asked what a propelling pencil was.

"I don't know, never heard of it," she murmured. An older woman who had introduced herself as Sarah, explained that it was a mechanical pencil.

"When the lead breaks you push a button on the top and a new lead comes down."

'That's clever, but how are we supposed to get that into a short story? That's plain weird' Helena thought, turning her attention back to the group leader.

"You can enter as many categories as you like, so have fun and I'll see you next time."

Later that evening Helena read through the competition entry rules, puzzling about how she could include the required propelling pencil in her short story. She jotted in her ideas notebook 'research propelling pencils', throwing away her biro in disgust when it ran out of ink. The pretty, hardback notebook was suffering from being stuffed in her bag and dragged out when she was struck by inspiration for a story or a scene. To tell the truth, it was battered, pages were torn and the ink was smudged. Although the intention was good, the notebook was home to a collection of vignettes which never made it into a complete story. Helena had joined the writer's group, hoping to finally write her first proper story.

Determined not to be put off by the requirement to include a propelling pencil in her story, Helena opened up her laptop and began to research online. Amazon offered a variety of plastic pencils with both black and coloured leads, but Helena skimmed over these. She was the kind of girl who enjoyed the finer things in life, her notebook and biro were homed in a vintage bag she'd bought on ebay, her favourite website. She often browsed the site, making up back stories for the items on sale. Who had worn the vintage 1930's cocktail dress or the Art Deco jewellery? What was their story? Their romance? Why was the current owner selling? Helena would weave her own stories letting her imagination fly wherever it chose to take her.

Clicking over to ebay she searched for propelling pencils and was immediately drawn to 'Collectible Pens and Writing Equipment.' Scrolling down the list her eyes lit up when she saw a vintage solid silver propelling pencil, engraved on the barrel of the pencil, was the letter H.

She quickly read the description. *Superb vintage solid silver Bakers Pointer propelling pencil hallmarked for Birmingham 1933 and bearing the makers mark of Edward Baker, the pencil is engraved with the order of the garter motto and the letter "H" so possibly belonged to a knight of the realm?*

It was clearly meant to be, the pencil had to be hers and she set an alarm on her phone to bid when the auction was about to end. Over the next 2 days she returned to the listing again and again. The price had crept up, but it was still just affordable. 30 seconds before the auction ended, she placed her winning bid.

The pencil arrived 3 days later and she unwrapped it reverently. This was a pencil with a history, who was 'H'? A wonderful back story began to emerge in her mind. She reached for her notebook. But no, that would not do at all. A pencil like this deserved a beautiful notebook. She would not use it until she had one.

A few days later she found the very thing in Petticoat Lane market whilst browsing the vintage stalls. Tooled, leather-bound books for journaling. Excited, she carefully selected her purchase and rushed home to begin her first entry in her Inspiration Book, as she had decided to call it.

Two hours later the page was blank. She tried to conjure up an image of the previous owner of the pencil. A Knight of the Realm. Had he been famous? Why had the pencil been sold on ebay? Another two hours later her mind was still blank and she'd given up trying to be inspired and decided to watch Love Island instead. Disappointed, she took the book and pencil to bed with her and left them on her bedside table, in case inspiration struck in the night. It didn't.

Helena was not going to be put off by this lack of inspiration. She polished the pencil carefully until the silver gleamed and stowed it safely in her vintage bag along with her new notebook. 'Inspiration will come' she thought 'I was meant to have this pencil.'

She held onto that thought for another week until the next writers' group session. Shyly smiling at the women she'd spoken to last time, they all took out their notebooks and pens. Helena proudly displayed her new, treasured possessions on the table for all to see. At that moment a late arrival burst through the door. "Sorry, is this the writer's group? Am I in the right place? Have you started"

Helena felt her breath leave her body, her heart began to race as she gazed at the face of the young man who flopped into the vacant seat next to her. He leaned across whispering in her ear, "hi, I'm Alistair." "Helena" she whispered back, unable to speak more than that one word coherently.

She found it hard to concentrate throughout the meeting, her fingers itching to pick up the pencil and start scribbling thoughts and ideas. Eventually she gave up the pretence of engaging with the group and picking up the pencil she allowed it to write. She couldn't have told you what she had written, it was as if a stream of consciousness filled the pages of her notebook.

At the end of the session Alistair disappeared as quickly as he arrived. She could remember every detail of his face, the colour of his eyes, hair, the strong jaw, trace of stubble on his chin. Who was he? Why had inspiration decided to strike at the moment he had sat next to her? With a sigh she carefully put the notebook and pencil away in her bag and walked out into the cold, dark night. She was tired, glad to go bed early, dropping the book and pencil on her bedside table. Her sleep was dreamless and uninterrupted by inspiration.

The following day Helena was busy at work. Lunch, as usual, was a snatched 15 minute break. The book and pencil had stayed safely stowed away in her bag all day, but how tempted she had been to read what she'd written the night before. It was not until she returned home, eaten her evening meal and settled comfortably on the sofa that she allowed herself to retrieve the notebook from her bag.

Her eyes began to widen as she read the notes she'd made. Here was a detailed description of the Knight of the Realm, his wife and family. The Knight had made some bad investments, when he died his family had been forced to sell some of his treasured possessions. His great grandson was a writer. She found she'd written a detailed description of Alistair and even sketched him, albeit rather crudely. Her spine tingled with excitement. At last, inspiration was coming through.

Astonished by what she'd written in her notebook, Helena sat at the kitchen table with a coffee and began to write a story on her laptop, every now and then referring to her notes. That night she fell asleep holding the pencil and her dreams were filled with characters, scenes and dialogue. Sleepily, she reached for the notebook and scribbled. The next morning a full page of the notebook was filled with her scribblings.

This pattern was repeated over the next few nights. If she fell asleep holding the pencil inspiration came through until her notebook was nearly half filled. 'I love this pencil, it's amazing' she thought, 'I'm never going to write with anything else.'

At the next writers group Helena was excited to share her experiences of writing with the propelling pencil. Just as they got started, Alistair rushed in, slipping into the seat next to her. Helena was slightly embarrassed about having described him in her notebook. She tried not to look at him as she used the pencil to make copious notes during the meeting. At the end of the evening he touched her arm gently as she was gathering up her things.

"I hope you don't mind, but could I look at the pencil you were using?"

Helena reluctantly handed it over, watching him to make sure he wasn't going to run off with it. "I know I'm being cheeky, but where did you get it?" he asked.

"Ebay," she replied "why?"

"I think it might have belonged to my great grandfather. It was passed down through the family after he died, sadly my mother had to sell it." He shrugged his shoulders. "Being a Knight of the Realm doesn't necessarily mean you're a good business man. I don't know how much you paid for it, but would you be willing to sell it to me? It would be nice to have it back in the family."

At that moment the group leader began to usher them out. "See you next time folks. Get your competition story entries in."

Alistair awkwardly shifted from one foot to the other.

"Look, I don't know about you, I could do with a drink, all this writing stuff makes me thirsty. Fancy joining me? There's a good pub near here. I promise I won't run off with your pencil." He grinned as he handed the pencil back to her.

Intrigued, Helena accepted the return of the precious silver pencil and together they walked to the pub chatting, getting to know each other a little. Helena shyly told him how she liked to know the history of an item when she bid for it on ebay. When they'd ordered drinks and food and were settled at the table Alistair asked to see the pencil again.

"I'm sure it's the same one, I remember seeing my grandmother scribbling away in her journal when I was a child. At the time I didn't realise she was writing children's stories. She used to read them to us when my sister and I were young. Mum says she used to read the same stories to her. It would be really lovely to have it back in the family."

"That's really sweet, but I've kind of fallen in love with this pencil." On impulse Helena showed him what she'd written at the previous session and the notes she'd made in the night. "Wow, that's incredible, you've described so much of my family. And me!" Helena felt her cheeks redden as she met his gaze.

"You know, you kind of remind me of my grandmother. I don't mean old and wrinkly" he laughed "that came out all wrong! I just feel like I've known you forever."

It was late when they left the pub. Alistair insisted on walking her home, telling her he lived very close to her flat. As Helena reached into her bag for her keys she realized she didn't have the pencil. "Oh no, I must have left it on the table" she wailed, "I must go back for it."

"The pub's closed now, I know the landlord, I'll get it for you tomorrow." Alistair smiled, hugged and kissed her quickly before walking off down the street feeling the heavy weight of the silver pencil in his pocket.

Helena's back story was good. He wondered how much the pencil would fetch on ebay next time.

TRAITor

Sophie wondered what her birthday gift from David would be this year. Her son usually presented her with a beautifully wrapped parcel containing a cardigan, scarf or perfume. His wife had good taste, but it would be nice if he made the effort to choose a gift himself. She sighed on hearing the doorbell ring, but pinned a smile on her face as she heard her son's voice.

"Happy birthday Mum, where are you? Hiding away in the kitchen as usual? Surprise, I've got something special for you." David appeared in the doorway, hands behind his back and an eager smile on his face. His expression reminded her of when he'd been about 11 and baked a birthday cake for her.

"Hello love, I'm here, just putting the kettle on. Dad's been in his man cave as usual. Have you got time for a coffee? I've made a cake." Sophie realized she was gabbling and stopped as David held out a parcel to her.

"Go on Mum, open it. I've outdone myself this year." He grinned as she carefully opened the parcel to reveal a plain cardboard box. Opening the box, she pulled out what looked like an ipad, a bit smaller and fatter, with a speaker like her Echo dot.

"Oh, that's nice dear. What is it? There's nothing on the box."

David beamed. "It's a brand-new prototype that my firm has developed. You know you complained about your Alexa thing, it doesn't always hear you properly or respond. This….."

Sophie almost expected to hear a drum roll as he paused before continuing.

"This is TRAIT. Our Thought Responsive Artificial Intelligence Technology. You don't have to talk to it, it responds to your thoughts. The Tbase will play music and do all the stuff Alexa does and much more. I'll connect the Tbase to your phone & computer and it will talk to you. I've just got to put a nano chip into the back of your neck and it'll start working."

"Well son, you've outdone yourself this year." Simon carefully picked up the device, "a prototype you say? This nano chip thingy, it's safe isn't it? You're not using your Mum as a guinea pig are you?"

"Yes Dad, of course it's safe. Though she's one of only a few people lucky enough to have one."

David picked up a gadget that looked rather like the device the vet had used to micro-chip their cat. "You'll just feel a slight pinch Mum, that's all. Turn round and I'll do it now."

The pinch was more like a stinging sensation, immediately Sophie could hear a buzzing sound in her head. Suddenly, the buzzing stopped and a voice spoke to her.

'Hello I'm TRAIT, I'm here to respond to your thoughts and needs. Would you like to give me a different name? Just think of my new name and we can begin.'

"Oh it's talking to me. In my head. It wants me to give it a name." Sophie touched the back of her head warily.

'Tell me your name, we are going to be friends for life.'

David was almost jumping up and down in excitement.

"It's working Mum, introducing itself. You just need to think your answers, no need to speak aloud. Go on, give it a name."

Sophie thought the first name that came into her head 'Harry, I'll call you Harry. I'm Sophie.'

'Harry, I like that name, it's much better than TRAIT. Hello Sophie, when you want me to listen to your thoughts, just begin with my name.'

"Oh this is strange, it's like Alexa, but it's in my head."

"Go on Mum, tell it to play some music. Think of what you'd like to hear."

"Er, well I quite like that Ed Sheeran. It can play him."

"Talk to it in your head, start with the name you've given it and then what you want it to do."

A few moments later the kitchen was filled with the sound of Ed Sheeran playing through the Tbase. Sophie smiled as she instructed Harry to play Happy Birthday by Stevie Wonder and the music changed instantly.

"Well son, that's pretty impressive. A prototype eh?" Simon looked enviously at the device. "Well done lad, well done."

Over the next few days Sophie gradually got used to her new friend Harry. She was delighted that as soon as she had a thought, Harry acted on it. Goods were added to her Ocado shopping App automatically. Phone calls were made. Reminder lists were created. Music played and even the TV channel changed, just by thinking about it.

Gradually she began to have conversations with Harry in her head. He was more responsive than Simon, who always seemed to have an excuse to disappear into his man cave.

'I wish he was more like the man I married' Sophie thought one night as Simon was getting ready for bed. 'We used to cuddle and talk in bed and sex was lovely. I miss it.' Simon gave her a perfunctory kiss and soon drifted off to sleep whilst Sophie lay awake next to him.

'Who would you prefer Simon to be like?' Harry's voice filled her head.

'Oh, I don't know, maybe Johnny Depp or George Clooney. Better still Colin Firth' she thought in reply.

'Imagine Colin Firth making love to you' Harry whispered in her head.

Suddenly her body was filled with waves of pleasure and she moaned as she writhed and gradually came to orgasm.

"Are you alright love? Have you got belly ache?" Simon propped himself up on his elbow, with a concerned expression on his face, "you look a bit strange."

Harry laughed in her head, 'if he only knew, Colin Firth just gave you an orgasm!'

Sophie nearly choked at Harry's words, "yes, I'm fine go back to sleep."

They were eating dinner the next night when Simon observed that she was more quiet than usual. Before Sophie could reply Harry spoke through the Tbase speaker.

"She wishes you were more like Colin Firth. Colin gave her a fantastic orgasm last night."

Sophie stopped eating, horrified. 'Shut up, Harry shut up' she thought as she pushed her chair away from the table and fled the room.

"And she's fed up with you spending so much time in your man cave. You don't talk to her enough. But it's okay, she's got me now." Harry's voice from the speaker echoed through the house.

Simon followed Sophie into the kitchen where she'd buried her face in a tea towel. Her shoulders were shaking as she tried to suppress laughter and tears.

"Is it right love, what that thing says? Are you fed up with me? I thought you didn't want me getting in your way in the kitchen." He tentatively stretched his hand out to touch her shoulder "I don't know what's wrong. Talk to me."

"It's a bit late for that. When did you ever offer to help in the kitchen? When did you last cook a meal for Sophie? Oh, I know, never. When did you last take her out for her birthday? You always expect her to cook for you, even on her birthday. But it's okay, she doesn't need you now, she talks to me. And I can give her better orgasms than you." Harry's voice went on and on filling the kitchen with all Sophie's unexpressed thoughts.

"But I didn't know. I thought it was what you wanted. Sophie, talk to me, shut that thing up will you."

'Harry, be quiet, stop talking. NOW.'

"Some of what Harry says is true, I do wish we'd talk more and do more things together. It would be nice if you helped me in the kitchen. I just feel like we're drifting apart. I miss our closeness. Our cuddles and love-making." Sophie stretched her hand out to Simon and he pulled her into his arms.

"Traitor, it's me you love now. You don't need him. Sophie. Please, you don't need him."

'Harry I told you SHUT UP, you're a machine, you're not real. I want my husband.'

But Harry's voice continued to scream through the speaker. "Traitor, traitor, it's me you want."

In desperation Sophie reached out for her heavy cast iron skillet. She smashed it down on the Tbase over and over until it was in pieces.

A few moments later the doorbell rang, and a burly policeman rushed into the kitchen.

113

"Are you alright in there? We just got a 999 call, someone called Harry, said he was being murdered."

"No officer, it was my Alexa thingy here. I've just destroyed it. Sorry."

"If you're sure you're alright? No one hurt is there?" asked the policeman eyeing the scattered remains of the Tbase.

"No, really we're fine, thank you." Simon ushered the officer out of the house.

All was quiet and Sophie breathed a sigh of relief.

'Traitor, you didn't think you'd get rid of me that easily did you?' whispered Harry.

Printed in Great Britain
by Amazon

48998924R00066